ALONG THE SALTWISE SEA

AS A. DEBORAH BAKER

Over the Woodward Wall
Along the Saltwise Sea

AS SEANAN McGUIRE

Middlegame
Dusk or Dark or Dawn or Day
Deadlands: Boneyard
Dying With Her Cheer Pants On
Laughter at the Academy

THE WAYWARD CHILDREN SERIES

Every Heart a Doorway
Down Among the Sticks and Bones
Beneath the Sugar Sky
In an Absent Dream
Come Tumbling Down
Across the Green Grass Fields
Seanan McGuire's Wayward Children, Volumes 1–3 (boxed set)

THE OCTOBER DAYE SERIES

Rosemary and Rue
A Local Habitation
An Artificial Night
Late Eclipses
One Salt Sea
Ashes of Honor
Chimes at Midnight
The Winter Long
A Red-Rose Chain
Once Broken Faith
The Brightest Fell
Night and Silence
The Unkindest Tide
A Killing Frost
When Sorrows Come

THE INCRYPTID SERIES

Discount Armageddon
Midnight Blue-Light Special
Half-Off Ragnarok
Pocket Apocalypse
Chaos Choreography
Magic for Nothing
Tricks for Free
That Ain't Witchcraft
Imaginary Numbers
Calculated Risks
Spelunking Through Hell

THE GHOST ROADS SERIES

Sparrow Hill Road

The Girl in the Green Silk Gown

Angel of the Overpass

THE INDEXING SERIES

Indexing

Indexing: Reflections

AS MIRA GRANT

THE NEWSFLESH SERIES

Feed

Deadline

Blackout

Feedback

Rise: A Newsflesh Collection (short stories)

THE PARASITOLOGY SERIES

Parasite

Symbiont

Chimera

Rolling in the Deep

Into the Drowning Deep

Final Girls

Kingdom of Needle and Bone

In the Shadow of Spindrift House

A TOM DOHERTY ASSOCIATES BOOK
New York

ALONG THE SALTWISE SEA

A. Deborah Baker

ALONG THE SALTWISE SEA

Edited by Lee Harris

A Tordotcom Book
Published by Tom Doherty Associates
120 Broadway
New York, NY 10271

www.tor.com

The Library of Congress Cataloging-in-Publication Data is available upon request.

ISBN 978-1-250-76828-5 (hardcover)
ISBN 978-1-250-76827-8 (ebook)

First Edition: October 2021

Printed in the United States of America

0 9 8 7 6 5 4 3 2 1

FOR SUZIE.

CONGRATULATIONS ON
SUCCESSFULLY SETTING SAIL.

ALONG THE SALTWISE SEA

ONE

ALONG THE IMPROBABLE ROAD

Once, in a time that was earlier than it is now and later than it might have been, later than the great ages of heroes and monsters, when quests were taught in school alongside the subjects we still have today, literature and swordsmanship, arithmetic and alchemy, science and the art of finding and fleeing from monsters, there were two children who had lived in the same ordinary town since the day that they were born. They had lived soft, swift, utterly ordinary lives, days blending into nights without any hint of the untidy impossible lurking around the edges, and their parents had looked at them and dreamed wholly ordinary futures devoid of magic or monsters or other complications.

These two children had lived their entire lives on

the same ordinary street, but as their parents were not friends—would, in fact, have recoiled from the thought of friendship that crossed class and societal lines with such flagrant disregard for keeping to one's own kind—and as they went to different schools, on opposite sides of their ordinary town, where they made the kind of friends their parents would approve of, they had never met one another, nor even so much as said hello in the public square. Avery was far too stuffy and preoccupied with neatness to be a good companion to Zib, who was in many ways what would happen if a large bonfire were somehow to be convinced to stitch itself into the skin of a little girl and go running wild across the fields of summer.

So Avery Alexander Grey and Hepzibah Laurel Jones had grown up, day by day and year by year, blissfully unaware that the person who would be the best of all their life's many friends, the person who would someday unlock the doorways to adventure, was less than a mile away that whole time. And then one day, one of the large pipes which carried water to the ordinary town took it upon itself to burst in the earth, causing an artificial flood and quite blocking the route that Avery ordinarily took to school. It was the sort of inconvenience that could have happened anywhere in the world, but which had, until recently, mostly left their ordinary little town alone. Adventure was against the civic bylaws, and best avoided, after all.

Avery's parents had raised him to be precise and rule-following, efficient and collected. He was a young boy who already looked well on his way to growing up to be a mortician, or perhaps a lawyer, if he could somehow be swayed to such a potentially frivolous position. He woke in the morning with hair that already seemed to have been combed into place, as if even the thought of untidiness were somehow worse than any other possible transgression. So when he saw that his route to school had been rendered impassable, he didn't return home, which would have involved his parents in his problems; he began looking for another way to get where he was going.

In contrast, Zib had been raised to view the world as a field to be frolicked through, as a forest of trees intended to be climbed. She had never once been told to be careful or slow down by any of the adults who mattered, not her parents, not her grandparents. Those commandments were frequently shouted by her teachers, but as she had been told they didn't count in the grand scheme of her own development, which included school only because her parents worked and couldn't watch her all day, and someone had to teach her how to spell and do her sums and all the other things she would need to know in order to be a great explorer when she grew up, she felt free to ignore them. When she found her way to school had been interrupted by a great gas explosion below the street, she saw it, not as an impediment, but as an opportunity for adventure, a chance to strike out on her own without technically disobeying the adults whose instructions ruled her days.

So it was that Avery and Zib, two children who had never, in the course of all their ordinary days, had the opportunity to meet, found themselves standing side by side on an unfamiliar stretch of sidewalk, looking in confusion at a wall that shouldn't have existed. It was at the end of the block, and there should have been another block ahead of them, and then another block, ordinary and predictable and marching one by one into the linear, expected future. Instead, the wall patiently persisted, each rough granite brick resting solidly upon the one below it, save for the bricks at the very base, which rested solidly upon the ground. Lichen and moss grew in patches on the stone, vital and somehow intrusive, like it had no business in a place as civilized as their hometown. Avery, who was rather more interested in carefully tended and cultivated gardens than Zib was, had never seen that sort of lichen growing anywhere in town, and Zib, who was rather more interested in woods and fields and wild places than Avery was, had never seen that sort of moss growing anywhere in the woods across from her house.

The wall did not belong there, of that there was no question; but the wall was unquestionably in front of them, solid and unyielding and right in the way of where they were meant to be walking. It was surrounded by blooming wildflowers. They poked out of the earth at its base, thriving where pavement should have blocked them from growing in the first place. They were very pretty flowers, and Zib thought her parents would have approved of them, even as she couldn't recognize them from any of the fields she knew. Like the rest of the wall, they were strange, and while she was a girl who normally favored strange things, they made her somehow uncomfortable, as if her failure to know and name them would come back to hurt her in the future.

Avery didn't recognize the flowers, either, but as they were not roses or daffodils or anything else tame and hence desirable, his failure to recognize them didn't bother him in the slightest. He assumed they were wild things of little value, and went back to staring at the stone, as if he could somehow will it to disappear. He had been here before, hundreds of times, and there had never been a wall between him and his destination. This one had no business where it was; it needed to go and be inexplicable elsewhere.

The wall, which must have known how to move in order to appear unbidden on their street, did nothing to yield or fade away. It continued to stand, as sturdy and implacable as if it had always been there, as if the town had grown up around it.

The two children, who were not yet friends, who did not yet even know each other's names, stood with their eyes on the wall and their minds whirling, hearts pounding in their chests.

Avery looked upon the wall and saw an offense, a distortion of the way the world was meant to be. If he had been asked, he would have said the wall was mocking him, something that shouldn't have been but was insisting on existing all the same.

Zib looked upon the wall and saw an opportunity, an adventure getting ready to begin and sweep her into the big and glorious future that she had always known was waiting for her. If she had been asked, she would have said the wall was beckoning her, making promises she was more than eager to believe.

Even the two children would have agreed that it was only natural that Zib was the first to begin to climb. She was wearing a skirt, mainly to quiet the protests of her teachers, who were forever asking if she didn't feel awkward and boyish when she wore trousers to school. As if there could be anything awkward about clothes that were *intended* for the climbing of trees! And if wearing trousers could make a girl into a boy, she supposed she'd never have been born, since her mother preferred trousers over everything else there was. The hem of her skirt had been patched and mended until it was more thread and knot than fabric. It bore the marks of much hard use. Her shoes were scuffed and her heels were worn and she simply looked like the sort of girl who would be happier going over an unfamiliar wall than standing placidly in front of it, an assumption that was well supported by the smile on her face as she climbed.

Avery did not have any mended tears in his perfectly pressed trousers, or on the cuffs of his button-down shirt. His shoes were perfectly shining, with scuff-free toes, as if he had only taken them out of the box this morning. Even his hair was combed like he was heading for a funeral. Had someone asked Zib in that moment whether he would climb the same wall she did, she would have replied that no, of course he wouldn't; whatever adventure was waiting on the other side of the wall, it was hers and hers alone.

She would have been terribly wrong. But no one can see the future clearly, not even the oracles with their crystal balls or the sea witches with their paper-chain tides, and so when she began to climb, he followed, unwilling to be left alone with the impossible.

When they reached the top of the wall, they found that there was no ordinary town on the other side; what should have been another ordinary street was only forest, stretching out for as far as the eye could see. They were both familiar with the tamer, more workaday *wood*. There were woods behind their houses, dark and tangled and filled with wild mysteries, but still somehow smaller and more domesticated than *forest*. This, though, this was *forest*. This was growth that had never known a woodsman, never feared an axe. These were trees that seemed to aspire toward tangling the sun in their branches and burning away to ash for the sheer delight of it all. Their branches rustled. Their leaves fluttered in a wind that was older, and colder than anything that had ever blown through the ordinary town where the children had lived their lives so far.

Still at the top of the wall, the children turned and looked back the way they had come, and when they saw that their homes—their homes, and with them, their parents, their beds, and everything they had ever known—were gone, they paused, both of them united for the first time. Then Zib toppled, end over end, onto the far side of the wall, and Avery climbed gingerly down after her, both of them committed by a combination of gravity and impossibility to the adventure that was ahead of them.

Ah, but all this is the beginning, and if we recount the entire story as it has been from the start, we will be here forever, never gaining ground, never going back to where we belong, victims and travelers on our own improbable road! That would not be the worst thing that has ever happened, for we would not be cold, or hungry, or wet, or lost as it was happening, but it is better to move forward, always, and we must be hurrying along. Hold fast, children, for things will happen quickly now.

In the forest on the other side of the wall, Avery and Zib found a world that was nothing like the one they had known all their lives so far. They found owls that could speak, and girls who burst into murders of crows, black wings beating against the sky. They found kings and queens, allies and enemies, and most of all, they found each other.

It can be easy, in this world, in any ordinary world, to walk through life assuming that what you already have is all that is worth having; that there are neither secrets nor mysteries important enough to be worth following onto a different path. But Avery and Zib learned, very quickly, that there were no mysteries worth the risk of losing their best and fastest friends: each other. For while they would come to care deeply for many of the people they met along their journey, for Avery, it would always be Zib, and for Zib, it would always be Avery. They were an alphabet unto themselves, A leading inexorably to Z, and they needed to hold fast to be completed.

But first: over the wall! Into the Up-and-Under, which had its own rules and its own laws and its own way of doing things, each one stranger and more perplexing than the last! They found themselves in the Forest of Borders to begin with, a strange place which edged upon every land within the Up-and-Under, although it could not be used to travel between them, and which seemed to take a certain smug pleasure in collecting travelers and dropping them into places they were ill equipped to survive, with their ideas of how the world worked and what "logic" meant. There they met the first of three owls, the great blue-feathered Meadowsweet, who started them upon the path to Quartz, who was a royal gnome, which is something like a man and something like a boulder and something like nothing either child had ever seen before.

It was Quartz who told the children that to return home, they would need to follow the improbable road until it led them to the Queen of Wands. But the improbable road was nothing so pedestrian as a path, nor so timid as a thoroughfare. It was not available to every casual Sunday stroller, did not appear for those who simply wished to go berry-picking at the forest's edge. It was a road with ideas and opinions of its own, and as such, could take time to coax out of hiding. It was also their only way to reach the Impossible City, where the Queen of Wands kept her court, and where other worlds could be easily accessed. Without the improbable road, they would have no adventure; they would simply have the long and painful process of learning to be citizens of a strange new land.

Upon finding the road, they lost Quartz, who was a creature of borders, and could not follow. They lost their footing in a mudslide, and found the first of their permanent allies on the other side: a girl in a short black dress made of crow's feathers, who had traded her name for a murder's wings, and who they would come to know as the Crow Girl. She told them they had left the lands of the King of Coins for the principality of the Queen of Swords, and because they had no way of knowing whether she told the truth or lied, they believed her. Believing can be easier than not believing, when there is nothing in the air to indicate a lie, and the Crow Girl was not lying, for lying took more imagination than a murder of crows bound in the body of a girl could carry on their soft black wings.

But onward! Ever onward! For a story already in progress must, by its very nature, continue to move forward, even as those who have just arrived at the theater are shrugging off their coats and searching for their seats. In the company of the Crow Girl, they traveled along the improbable road, and met the Bumble Bear, who had not been born a monster, but who had become one in the service of the Queen of Swords, who was often crueler than she had the need to be. He took the shine from Avery's shoes as a toll for their passage, and if Zib didn't understand the importance of that moment, Avery did, and would mourn it all the rest of his days.

The children discovered two treasures: a skeleton key that would allow them to bypass the protectorate of the King of Cups, and the flavor fruit, a wonderful thing created by the Queen of Wands when she had to give up her place as maiden of the summer and take up the mantle of the Impossible City. Soon they met Broom, next of the great owls, who warned them to be careful of their choices and to stay on the road. Heeding neither of these warnings, Avery chose to leave Zib, and Zib chose to leave the road, and they found themselves in possession of a lock for their key, given to Zib by the impetuous Queen of Swords. The lock opened onto a shortcut gone wrong, which dropped them, not into the safe fields of the Queen of Wands, but into the frozen wastes of the King of Cups.

There they met Niamh, a drowned girl from a city locked deep below the ice, who had become separated from her people when the winter arrived, and who wandered seeking only to avoid the King and Page until she could go home again, if that day ever arrived. Niamh offered what aid she could before the Page of Frozen Waters interfered. Zib fell from the high, frozen cliffs and was lost, or would have been, had the last of the great owls, Oak, not come and carried Zib away. His intention was to free her, but the Page of Frozen Waters appeared again, presenting Zib as a great treasure to the King of Cups. He caged her, and as feathers swelled beneath her breastbone and her limbs ached to burst into crows, Avery and the Crow Girl sought to find her.

People who believe they have a right to power will always find ways of making monsters from those they perceive as weaker than themselves. There is not always malice in this act, but that does not make it innocent, or forgivable. It is still betrayal, however kindly it is proposed, and had Zib been a little less fortunate in her friends, had Avery been a little less clever or the Crow Girl a little less brave, she would have been lost forever.

The riverbeds are lined with the bones of children whose adventures ended too soon, done in by the words "a little less," which are always uttered by those who see anyone unafraid of their own choices as too wild, too rambunctious, too *much*.

Avery and the Crow Girl released Zib from her confinement, and the three fled the King and Page, taking refuge with the great owls, who confirmed something the Crow Girl had told them by mistake: that the Queen of Wands had disappeared, and without her, the Up-and-Under was in great danger, for balance cannot be maintained when an entire season has stepped out of sight. They could not enter the Impossible City with Niamh, for a drowned girl is an all-too-possible thing, and the City did not want her for its own.

Avery and Zib were both new, for different reasons, to the feeling of having friends, but even so, both of them understood leaving a friend behind was a difficult thing to forgive. So they knew the Impossible City was not for them. They would take her with them on their journey to find the Queen of Wands, who must need finding, for she was missing, after all.

And so this is where, after so much reminding of what has come before, we enter the story, which is already in progress, and has been in progress for a long, long time. Two children, both a little muddy and unkempt, but one with clothing that is still untorn, still largely perfectly pressed, and the other with a mended skirt and hair so wide and wild it looks as if it hungers to consume the entire world, walk down a road of glittering, glistening, improbable bricks, alongside a taller girl with feathers barely contained beneath the surface of her skin and another near their own age who leaves a trail of dampness behind her as she walks. They are on their way to something glorious.

They don't yet know what it is. Let us follow them, and be there when they find out.

TWO

HOW MANY CHILDREN CAN FIT IN A BUCKET?

Zib had never thought, once in her life, that she might regret being barefoot. Barefoot had always seemed to her to be a person's natural state, something to be coveted and aspired to, especially when parents and teachers and other adults who had forgotten the simple joy of grass between their toes yelled for her to put her shoes back on. People who wore shoes too often got soft, their feet growing tender, until they could barely walk down the driveway without yelping in pain. She never wanted to be one of those tender-footed people, unable to run out the door without stopping to strap her feet into confining leather cages.

Now, after what felt like hours of walking along the improbable road, she was starting to wonder if they might not have had a point. Her feet ached and throbbed until they took up almost the entirety of her thoughts, pushing everything else into a corner of her mind. She was on a fabulous adventure, doing things she had never done or considered doing before, talking to owls, walking with drowned girls, and here she was, thinking about how much her feet hurt.

But as much as she wanted to raise her voice in complaint, to demand that everything be rendered soft and soothing and kind, she knew that Avery had to feel worse than she did. She was a climber of trees and a runner in fields; she had spent her life to date barefoot more often than not. Avery couldn't say any of those things. Avery was a solid, sensible creature, accustomed to solid, sensible shoes, and his feet were as tender as any adult's. Zib couldn't even imagine a life with as little running and climbing as the one he'd lived so far; it seemed to her that it must have been a terribly dull thing indeed.

The Crow Girl had tired of walking some time ago, and had burst into birds as easily as anything, taking to the air in a great swirl of black feathers and beating wings. She perched in the bushes and trees they passed, rested her talons on the shoulders and heads of her companions, and was light enough, being made mostly of hollow bones and longing, that none of them objected, not even Avery. Niamh looked positively amused each time a crow settled on her shoulder, only to take off and flap away in disgust as the water that perpetually dripped from the drowned girl's hair dampened its feathers.

The fields to either side of the improbable road were green and verdant, dotted with patches of the most beautiful wildflowers Zib had ever seen. They seemed to come in every color of the rainbow, and a few colors the rainbow had forgotten. Apart from the Crow Girl, there were no other birds, although butterflies and fat, rainbow-striped bees flitted from bloom to bloom. They were the sort of fields designed by the universe for running through and rolling in, and the possibility of bee sting or bramble only made them more appealing. Or would have, under ordinary circumstances. Zib looked at the fields and realized she had no desire to run through them.

Suddenly overcome with the unjustness of it all, Zib sat heavily and abruptly in the grass by the side of the road. "I'm *tired,*" she declared. "I'm *tired* and my feet hurt, and I thought we were only going to walk for long enough to find someplace to stay the night, not for forever!" She raked her hands through the tangled, curled, riotous mass of her hair, dislodging several twigs and a pencil, and flopped backward into the grass. "I can't do it. I can't walk any more than I've walked already."

There was a rustling of wings and a rushing sound as the Crow Girl came back together and landed with a thump at the edge of the improbable road, looking down on Zib. "You said you'd never been to the

Up-and-Under before, and you don't know *anything*, so I suppose I thought you were telling the truth."

"I *was* telling the truth!" Zib protested peevishly, and threw an arm across her eyes, blocking out both the light and the sight of the Crow Girl's clever, inquisitive eyes, set as they were in a face that was just barely too sharp to pass for human.

"But you can't have been, or you wouldn't be so sure that you've gotten where you're supposed to be going!" The Crow Girl stepped back. "I guess you must know what to do when the brambles wake up and come to carry you away."

"Brambles?" asked Zib, who had seen a wall of brambles spring out of the ground to keep Quartz from setting foot on the improbable road all the way back at the Forest of Borders, at the beginning of their increasingly exhausting adventure.

"Brambles," said Niamh, a hint of amusement in her voice. "They sleep during the day, but when the sun goes down, all these fields will belong to them. You don't want to be out in the open when they decide to take what's theirs."

"I think I can walk a little more," said Zib, springing to her feet. Avery, who had been leaning forward, taking advantage of the break, offered her a pale smile. He didn't have it in him to make a scene, not without substantially more motivation than aching feet—if ever there was a child who had internalized "children should be seen and not heard," it was Avery—but that didn't mean he couldn't be grateful when a scene came along to save him. Scenes had a lot of power like that. Zib stepped up beside them, and the two children resumed their plodding trek along the improbable road.

Niamh, whose feet did not get tired because they were forever halfway frozen through, looked at the children and frowned. She could see that they were suffering, and they had been good friends to her; if she wanted to be a good friend to them, it seemed only reasonable that she find some way to make their suffering less. They were still close enough to the Impossible City to be in the protectorate of the Queen of Wands, where fire and inspiration reigned supreme. Fire lessened her ability to help, but inspiration made so many things possible. She looked to the Crow Girl.

"Can we call on the owls to help us?" she asked.

"The owls have gone back to their nests, their own places, and they have better things to do than whisk a bunch of vagabonds along a road," said the Crow Girl, somewhat anxiously. "It's better that way. They're so much bigger than I am, they fill me with the need to harry, to make them fly away from my territory. I don't think that would be a good thing. Harrying the owls might be the last thing I ever decided to do."

Niamh, who lacked a corvid's instinct to protect, nodded as understandingly as she knew how to do. "Yes," she said. "It would be best if you didn't do that." Going back would change nothing; it would only put two barefoot children through even more miles of road, and deposit them all at the border of a city they couldn't enter. Losing the Crow Girl to an angry owl's talons would change everything.

She looked toward the horizon. It was no different than the slice of field where they were standing, green and delicately sloping as it faded into the distance. There were no buildings to break the inherently gentle view. There were no trees or towers or mountains. Viewed from where she stood, the principality of the Queen of Wands could have been nothing more or less than an unending field.

The children would collapse long before they reached that horizon. There were no clear water sources here, no bonberry bushes or flavor fruit trees. Between Avery and the Crow Girl, they had three flavor fruits, and one of those was already half-gone. The improbable road was supposed to help them get where they were going, but right now, it didn't seem all that interested in anything but distance.

Niamh kicked the bricks in front of her with vicious swiftness. "Hey," she said, voice clear and carrying. "We can't walk forever. Human children get tired. Human children need water, and soft places to rest. What do you think you're doing?"

It was improbable that a road should listen when lectured, and even more improbable that the road should be able to do anything about the lecture. Roads were, by and large, stationary, unyielding things, staying where they were put, following a single, predictable path until they were worn away by weather, traffic, and time. But this was the improbable road, which existed primarily to do things that roads weren't meant to do. Sunlight glittered off the bricks. Zib, who was no longer picking up her feet quite as well as she had been when they'd started walking, cried out as her toe hooked on a brick and she pitched forward, catching herself on hands and knees before her face could meet the ground. Avery hurried to help her back to her feet, and in the process, she looked back the way they'd come, and gasped.

"Avery, look!" she said. "The city's gone!" She shook off the hand that still held her elbow as if it were nothing at all, and started walking in the other direction. "The city's gone, and there's a well!"

Somehow, the presence of the well was even more exciting than the absence of the city. Wells meant water, after all, and water meant a way to cool and soothe her aching feet.

Avery followed more slowly. He had seen wells before—of course he had, his parents could only shelter him so much from the world—but he had never actually used one. In his world, drinking water was delivered to the house three times a week by the water-carrier, and washing water came out of the sink, carried by buried pipes that half his classmates happily drank from. His father didn't trust the water system yet, said it was too new and complicated and that some things shouldn't be changed as long as they were working properly. Only a fool would drink water that had traveled so far underground, trapped in shadows, spinning inward on itself and turning sour. Well water was supposed to be an acceptable substitute for drinking, if you were out in the country and didn't have any alternatives.

Well, they were truly out in the country now. The Impossible City, which was the only city he'd even heard of in the Up-and-Under, was gone, and they had nothing left to their name but fields, the improbable road, and now the well that Zib was hurling herself against, gripping the edge as she knocked the air out of her own body with the impact.

Zib had more experience with wells than Avery did. Her father had been born on a farm, and his parents still owned the property. She spent every summer with them, running feral through the fields of corn and strawberries, getting twigs tangled in her hair and stealing warm eggs out from under broody hens. She felt around until her hands found the handle on the well's side, and then she began to crank, reeling in the rope and the bucket at its end.

When it finally came into view, it was sleek and silver, with not a hint of rust or tarnish, and filled with water so clear and perfect that Zib knew even without tasting it how sweet it would be. She reached for it with shaking hands, as the others walked up behind her.

"This is a wishing well," said Niamh, sounding pleased. "They're generally harmless, and not home to misplaced river hags or unspeakable curses."

"They grant wishes?" asked Avery, as Zib pulled the bucket toward herself.

"No, not at all," said Niamh. "What a queer notion, a well granting wishes! Might as well ask for grass to set the table, or clouds to control the weather. No, wishing wells are wells that have been wished for. They go where they're most needed. Or where they're brought. I suspect the improbable road went and fetched this one for us." She gave the bricks at her feet a hard look.

The improbable road twinkled in the sunlight, silent and smug.

Zib grasped the bucket and brought it to her mouth, taking her first sip of the cleanest, sweetest water she had ever tasted. It was also freezing cold, and she gasped, losing her grip and dumping the contents of the bucket down her front, drenching herself and rinsing the dust and dirt of her adventures away. Squealing in dismay, she released the empty bucket, which fell back into the well with a noisy splash.

Avery looked at his sodden companion and laughed, barely catching it in his hand. Zib glared at him. He laughed harder, unable to keep it penned inside. Zib lost her glare and grinned. She was cold, yes, but she was growing accustomed to being cold; the Up-and-Under seemed to take a sour pleasure in drenching them at every turn, like its ultimate goal was to make sea creatures of them all. She was cold, and she was closer to clean than she had been in days, and the water numbing her toes made it easier for her to stand up straight without complaining.

"Do you want some water?" she asked, and Avery nodded, and she began cranking up the bucket again, leaning into the movement, so that it happened quickly enough to be worth doing.

The Crow Girl leaned over the edge of the well, peering down into its shadowy depths. "What's down there?" she asked.

"Water," said Zib. "Frogs, maybe. Not fish, usually. Fish can't get enough to eat in a well."

"Do frogs?"

"Frogs fall in and then they can't get out," said Zib.

"Does that mean the water is full of dead frogs?"

It was an unsettlingly squishy question. Zib hesitated before she saw the flicker of alarm in Avery's eyes and said, firmly, "No. If there are any dead frogs, they sink to the bottom, and we're only taking water from the top. It tastes wonderfully fine. Not like frog at all."

"I'm going down to look," said the Crow Girl, and burst into birds before spiraling into the well, a whirlwind of black wings flying down into the darkness. Zib laughed as she continued to reel in the bucket. Avery peered nervously after the Crow Girl.

"Can she fly with wet wings?" he asked.

Niamh nodded. "She can fly in a hurricane. All Crow Girls can, especially when they have their whole murder in one place. Don't worry about her."

The bucket inched slowly into view, a crow riding on its rim.

"Get off of there," scolded Zib. "You don't weigh

much, but water does, and I don't need the bucket to be any heavier than it already is."

The crow hopped off the bucket with an obliging squawk, fluttering its wings as it moved to the rim of the well. Zib assumed it was a girl crow, although she'd never asked; maybe the murder was made up of girl crows *and* boy crows, and it didn't matter. It felt like it should matter. It also felt like a deeply personal question that she had no business asking. Feelings were sometimes difficult.

Taking the bucket off the hook that held it, Zib offered it to Avery. He looked at the water warily, as if he expected the rumored frogs to appear and start croaking to him about their days. Zib sighed, still holding out the bucket.

"Don't you want something to drink?" she asked. "Because if you don't, I'm pouring this back in the well. It's heavy. I don't want to stand here holding it forever."

"I don't want to drink a frog," he said, still studying the water. Finally seeming to satisfy himself that there weren't any frogs in the bucket, he reached out and took it gingerly from her hands, lifting it toward his mouth.

The water was as sweet as Zib had said. It tasted better than fresh milk or pop from the corner store. He would never have believed that water could be so delicious, or leave him so eager for more. When he had drunk so much his belly felt fat and distended with water, he lowered the bucket and offered it back to Zib. "Here."

"I feel better now," said Zib, before taking a swig from the remaining water in the bucket and offering it to Niamh. Niamh took the bucket and drank deeply, closing her eyes. She didn't bother checking for frogs. She also didn't bother breathing. Both Avery and Zib watched with wide, awed eyes as the drowned girl finished the contents of the bucket in a single long gulp, lowering it to reveal wetted lips and flushed cheeks.

"That was lovely," she said, placing the bucket back onto the hook before climbing into it, giving the rope an experimental tug. She looked back to Zib and Avery. "Well? Come along."

"You're in a bucket," said Zib, with careful delicacy.

"Yes, I had noticed," said Niamh. "I got into it on purpose. You can come into it too, if you would like."

"I don't think it's big enough," said Zib.

"This is a wishing well," said Niamh, patiently. "The bucket is exactly as large as we need for it to be."

"Oh, then, I've never been in a bucket before," said Zib, and pulled herself up onto the well's edge before reaching for Niamh. The drowned girl took her hands and tugged her gently forward, and Zib tumbled into the bucket, finding herself seated quite securely on the lip, with her bare feet against the cool wood of the bottom.

It was quite the most comfortable seat she'd had in hours, and so she turned a sunshine smile on Avery, and said, "Come on, Avery. We'll all fit in this bucket if we try, and it feels so nice."

Avery, who had noticed the Crow Girl's failure to return from the bottom of the well, and who had a slightly more developed sense of narrative structure than Zib did, having always been rather more interested in staying in his room to read, bit his lip and looked at the bucket. "If I get in the bucket, will the rope break and drop us all to the bottom of the well?"

"No," said Niamh. "I promise, the rope won't break."

"All right, then." Carefully, he climbed up onto the edge of the well and followed Zib's path to the bucket itself, tumbling in after the two girls. It was as comfortable as Zib had said, and as large as Niamh had: there was no possible way the three of them, even as small as they were, could have fit in the bucket, but there they all were, and there the bucket was, and when Avery looked at himself, he didn't feel as if he was any smaller.

"Everyone comfortable?" asked Niamh. "Have a good grip? Excellent." She looked to the edge of the well, where the single crow to have made the trip back up to the surface was sitting. "If you would be so kind," she said.

The crow hopped onto the crank that allowed the bucket to be raised and lowered, and, with one steady kick, sent it spinning, and sent the bucket, with all three passengers, plummeting down into the darkness.

Zib squealed. Niamh laughed. Avery screamed. And those reactions tell you everything there is to know about those three children in that single, frozen moment.

Then the bucket hit the surface of the water with a splash, and everything was silence. With a caw that was virtually a laugh, the crow tucked its wings in against its body and plummeted after the others, down into the darkness of the well.

THREE

WHERE BRAMBLES STEAL THE SKY

Niamh tumbled out of the bucket when it hit the water, drifting downward with her eyes open and her arms spread wide. When she was so far below the surface that she could no longer see the moment when the small bubbles trickling from her nose reached the air and rejoined it, she took a deep breath, filling her belly and lungs with water, and began to swim leisurely toward the dim light above her.

She broke the surface and spat a jet of water into the air, as elegant and untroubled as a stone fountain. Avery and Zib, who were still clinging to the bucket's edge, shrieked in unified surprise. Niamh offered them a lazy smile and spat another stream of water.

"You said the rope wouldn't break!" shouted Avery.

"It didn't break," said Niamh. "The Crow Girl turned the crank."

Avery and Zib looked around, their eyes adjusting to the new darkness. The stone walls around them were covered in crows, their talons clamping down on every little jut and jag in the rock. Their eyes were bright and glittering in the dim light.

"You told her to. Why?" asked Zib. "You had to know we'd fall."

"Yes, but this is water, and I'm stronger in the water," said Niamh. "You were saying you wanted to stop and rest. Where better to rest than at the bottom of a well?"

"I can think of a lot of places," said Avery. "Sunshine places. Dry places."

"I wouldn't like to rest in a desert," said Zib dubiously.

"I never said anything about a desert!"

"But deserts are dry, sunshine places," said Zib, in a tone which implied Avery was being unreasonable. "I'm so tired and sore right now that being in the water seems like about the best thing that could happen." And with that, she pushed herself off the edge of the bucket and joined Niamh in the well with a quiet splash. Shivering, she leaned back to float. "It would be nice if the water were just a little bit warmer, though."

"Cold well water is one of life's sweetest pleasures," said Niamh. "It wouldn't be nice to everyone else if we warmed up the well."

"But we're already swimming in the well," said Zib.

"How is that nice to everyone else? If they pull the bucket back up, they'll get Avery, and Zib-flavored water. I don't think they want either of those things."

"All will be well, if you'll excuse the pun," said Niamh patiently. "Avery, come in the water. It's nice here."

"I'd rather stay dry," said Avery, looking at the dark water with mistrust.

Zib laughed, splashing at him. "Only you would think you could stay dry at the bottom of a well," she said. "Wells aren't where you go to stay dry, not unless a drought is happening, and when there's a drought, everything is bad. There's no drought happening here."

Avery started to answer, and then froze, paling, as the bucket rocked violently beneath him. "Stop kicking the bucket," he said.

Zib blinked. "What?"

"I said, stop kicking the bucket. I don't like it, it's not funny, and friends shouldn't do things just to be mean." The bucket rocked even more violently. Avery clutched the handle, glaring at Zib. "I asked you to stop!"

"You didn't ask, you told, and I'm not doing anything!" said Zib. She held her hands up in illustration, dipping lower in the water. "I wouldn't!"

Avery frowned, and switched his suspicious gaze to Niamh, who was drifting in the water on the other side of the well, out of reach of the bucket. Again, he started to speak.

This time he was interrupted by the bucket—Avery and all—being jerked abruptly under the water, leaving only a flurry of bubbles behind. Zib jerked upright, splashing and flailing as she tried to find some trace of him in the dark well.

"Avery?" she exclaimed. "Avery, where are you?"

The crows on the walls began to croak and caw, creating a jolly ruckus that bounced back and forth between the stone and the water, until it was so loud it was almost deafening. Under the circumstances, it was understandable when Zib failed to notice Niamh vanishing below the water, dragged down by something unseen.

The crows continued to call as Zib looked frantically around. They called louder when something wrapped around her ankles and jerked downward, hauling her into the drenched, freezing darkness.

The water calmed in the absence of an upset, thrashing girl. The crows continued to yell. Then they pulled themselves together, becoming another girl, this one longer of limb and dressed in black feathers. The Crow Girl dropped into the well with the force of a flung stone.

She didn't surface again.

Beneath the water, Zib was yanked along, mouth open in a silent scream and trailing bubbles. Niamh was visible a little bit ahead of her, pale, waterlogged skin seeming to almost glow in the dimness. No bubbles trailed from her mouth or nose. She might as well have been a corpse, carried along by the current.

Avery, who had been the first taken, was entirely out of view.

Down and down and down they traveled, helpless against the force that had ensnared them, until they broke through the bottom of the aquifer, a shimmering, pearlescent veil of liquid, and into open air. Zib gasped, choking out the water in her lungs even as she greedily replaced it with air. Niamh weathered the transition without visible distress. They plummeted toward the ground, which was covered in a writhing mass of fleshy green fronds that smelled of salt and sunlight. Avery was already there, pillowed by the green, not moving.

The pair struck down. The Crow Girl came tumbling after them, narrowly managing not to land on Zib. She squawked and spat water before turning to the human child and asking, "Did you pull me down?"

"No," rasped Zib, in a voice as waterlogged as a kitchen sponge on cleaning day. "I think the plant did that." She indicated the writhing green mass beneath them. It wasn't grabbing or pulling anymore, or trying to eat them. That was enough of an improvement that she didn't want to question it, not really.

Niamh crawled over to Avery, who was sprawled alongside the remains of the bucket. The rope had snapped at some point during his descent, and its frayed end rested on his chest, like a tether to nowhere. Reaching out, she gingerly shook his shoulder.

"Peace, Avery," she said. "I know drowning, and

you're not drowned. Open your eyes and come back where you belong."

Avery remained still and silent for several seconds more before he coughed, water coming out of his mouth, sat up, and vomited into the bucket. He took a great, shuddering breath, leaned over the bucket, and vomited again.

"That's surprisingly tidy of you," said Niamh, in an approving tone. "Never throw up on anyone you haven't been introduced to. I would normally suggest not sitting on anyone you haven't been introduced to, either, but it's a bit late for that, and since this charming individual tried to drown us all, it seems like a little sitting-on is simply tit for tat."

"Individual?" asked Avery blearily.

Several of the nearest green fronds lifted up and waved gingerly in the air, for all the world like the fingers of a vast hand folding over themselves. Avery screamed.

Zib jerked around to face him, and followed his scream with one of her own, much higher and shriller. The Crow Girl burst into birds, all of them cawing loudly and frantically as they flew around the cavern. Avery kept screaming, and so did Zib. Niamh rolled her eyes.

"Screaming isn't going to help or change anything," she said. "No matter how loud you get, the facts remain the same. I've never encountered noise-soluble facts, although I suppose they must exist. If someone has a headache, and you scream in their ear, the fact is that their headache may get worse, and you may get punched, very hard."

They, and the green thing, were in what looked like a natural cave carved out of the side of a vast stone outcropping. The walls were remarkably smooth, offering no real perches for the crows now whirling through the air. The ceiling, the parts of it that weren't a rainbow-wrapped wall of water, was made of the same stone, and was equally smooth. Only the ground differed, consisting of wide patches of glittering sand between the green fronds.

The fronds were still waving frantically, although it was difficult to say whether or not that had anything to do with all the screaming. Zib climbed to her feet and went stomping barefoot through the green to Avery's side, spreading her arms as if posture would help her to scream even louder. A dozen or so crows came to roost on her, cawing and flapping their wings. Zib kept screaming, but she didn't sound alarmed anymore. She was almost smiling, and seemed to be screaming for the sake of making a big and increasingly joyous noise.

Avery stopped screaming and clutched his ears. "Stop, stop, *stop*," he wailed.

Zib stopped screaming. The crows stopped cawing. Not all at once; it took a while for the ones who were whirling around the cavern to realize that the sound was dying out, and close their beaks accordingly. But the ones on her arms stopped quickly, and the silence spread out from there, like the ringing of an unhearable bell.

"Where *are* we?" demanded Avery, lowering his hands and turning toward Niamh.

"Well, this is helpful kelp," said Niamh, nudging the green thing with her toe. "It grows along the beaches of the Saltwise Sea. I've always thought it was so helpful because it's a border creature, and all border creatures know, on some level, that they belong to the Forest of Borders, which is a helpful place."

Avery, who remembered the Forest of Borders all too well and had his own opinions about how helpful it was, said nothing.

Zib waded through the fronds, arms still held up for the crows, and asked, "How was it helpful for the kelp to drag us all that way underwater? We could have drowned!"

"Not all of us," said Niamh patiently. "I couldn't have drowned, even if I'd been trying my very hardest. Drowning is like being born; you can only really do it the once. Any time you try after that, you might manage a parody of the first time, but you'll never *actually* do it."

"I'm not a drowned girl," said Zib, tone going irritable. She finally shook the crows off her arms, and they all came together a few feet away, consolidating into the form of the Crow Girl. Zib put her hands on her hips. "The owls speak riddles," she said. "You're not one of the owls. You're supposed to be our friend.

So tell us what's going on, and why we're here, and why it was worth losing the improbable road."

The improbable road can always be found again by travelers in the Up-and-Under. It's improbable that a road should be accessible no matter where someone is standing, and any improbability in the Up-and-Under feeds into the road's design. Perhaps that was why Niamh looked at Zib, and sighed, before saying, with the utmost patience, "It's not lost. It's just not here right now." She paused before adding thoughtfully, "*We're* lost. The road is exactly where it needs to be."

Zib stared at her. The Crow Girl cleared her throat before asking, "If it's help-kelp, why did it grab us before? We didn't need any help."

"Ah, but maybe it thought we did," said Niamh. "Most people don't seek shelter in the bottom of wells, after all."

"So it thought we were in trouble?" asked Zib. "How can a plant think anything? Plants don't have brains."

"And roads can't move, and flocks of crows can't become girls when they want to enjoy the luxury of thumbs," said Niamh. "You need to break your addiction to the idea that anything is impossible. Things don't have to be possible to be true."

Zib was fairly sure that "not true, not real" was part of the definition of "impossible," but Niamh was right: she had seen so many impossible things since falling into the Up-and-Under that it was silly for her to start drawing arbitrary lines now. "I'm sorry, Mr. Kelp," she said, stepping off the fronds and leaning down to give one a gentle pat. "We weren't in any trouble, but you didn't know that, and you didn't drown any of us, not really. As long as you don't do that again, we can be friends."

A few fronds lifted carefully into the air. One of them stroked Zib's hair. She laughed.

Avery finally let go of the bucket. Niamh wrinkled her nose and picked it up, moving it away from the helpful kelp, which had already been through enough and didn't really need to be doused in someone else's sick. Not when it had only been trying to help. This was a form of compassion on her part, and while it may have been somewhat misplaced, it was in no way misguided. The two things are not always the same, however much some people may make them out to be.

The Crow Girl, shivering in the dim cave and her wet feathers, looked around as she rubbed her arms, and asked, "Can the help-kelp help us out of here? I don't think we can go back up through the well."

"No, probably not," agreed Niamh, looking at the pearlescent water hanging above them. Of the four, she was the best suited to such a journey, and even she failed to find any real appeal in it. Upward through an aquifer was an adventure unto itself, and only she could breathe underwater. "We're here now, I suppose. We should go and find out where here is."

The kelp gathered itself, pulling away from the

sand and out from under their feet and twisting into a single tall column that resembled nothing as much as it did a tree. It pointed deeper into the cave with all of its kelp-frond "branches."

"Is that the way out?" asked Zib.

The "tree" shivered in what looked like agreement before untwisting and falling back to the sandy ground.

"Can we really trust a pile of seaweed?" asked Avery.

"Do we have a choice?" countered Zib. "At least my feet don't hurt anymore. Come on! Let's see where we are!" And she started walking, in the direction the kelp had indicated. Niamh and the Crow Girl followed, until the three of them were walking off across the sand and Avery was standing alone with the help-kelp, which sprawled motionless around him.

"Don't leave me here!" shouted Avery.

Niamh turned, walking backward as she said, "And why shouldn't we? None of us want to be here anymore, and you haven't suggested anything better than finding the exit from this cave. Help-kelp wouldn't send us off to be devoured by some monster in the shadows. That isn't in its nature. We're going outside. Come or stay, that's up to you."

Avery frowned at her, trying to imitate the powerful frown he'd seen his father wear when something wasn't going the way he wanted it to. Niamh looked back at him, unperturbed. With a sigh, he stepped away from the kelp and ran after the others, feet slapping against the sand. Niamh nodded to him.

"See? Sometimes it's better to go and see what can be seen than it is to stay exactly where you are."

"Just because you outnumber me, that doesn't mean you get to tell me what to do," he said.

Niamh blinked. "I didn't tell you what to do. Hepzibah did, a little bit, when she told you to come on, but no one made you listen. No one can make you do anything. No one except for you. But if we can't tell you what to do, that means you can't tell us what to do, either. That's what fairness looks like. We don't make your choices, and you don't make ours."

"But . . . but you're bullying me into going along with what you want," said Avery.

"No," said Niamh. "We're not. We're just leaving. You can leave with us, or you can be alone without us. That isn't bullying. Now, we *could* bully you, but this isn't what bullying looks like. This is just what leaving looks like."

Avery frowned again, thoughtfully this time, and not like a frown was the quiet second side of a fist. He kept walking, the sand cool between his toes, and thought about what Niamh had said. As an only child, he had had plenty of time to get used to the idea of being outnumbered by his parents, who decided almost everything according to majority rule, and who had raised him to be a biddable child. When the two of them together wanted something, well, that was what was going to happen, and it didn't matter if he wanted it at all!

But this wasn't like that, because his friends had been happy to leave him behind if that was what he wanted to do. Their unwillingness to yield to his desires in what was, really, a fairly straightforward situation, with only two choices at hand, wasn't the same as his mother telling him what to wear so they could go see his grandmother, who didn't like him very much and always smelled, in a subtle but undeniable way, of sour milk and cod. This was more akin to his mother declaring that *she* was going to go see his grandmother, but he was welcome to stay home if he preferred, keeping himself company with his books and building blocks and thoughts.

He found he liked this better.

Avery didn't have much experience with making friends. The other children at his school had a tendency to think of him as too boring and straitlaced to be worth playing with, and he had never pressed the issue, preferring the company of teachers and the librarian, none of whom wanted him to run around and get dirty the way the other children did.

Well, he was learning about getting dirty now! The Up-and-Under seemed to have a particular dislike of his being clean. He had been bathed in mud and dropped in sand and doused and frozen and lost the shine out of his shoes before losing the shoes themselves. And in a place like this one, he was direly afraid that losing the shine meant more than it would have back at home, where shoe polish existed for sale in every general shop. Here, the loss seemed strangely permanent, like something that should have been considered much more carefully.

Not that he had made the choice in the first place, and not that Zib understood what it was to put value on the shine of a pair of shoes. He held the thought without anger, even though he had been angry with her when the bargain was first made; she had, after all, given away something that was *his*, and not hers to bargain with. But she hadn't done it out of malice. She had been trying to preserve them both from the Bumble Bear, who had become a monster when the Queen of Swords had need of one, and had never remembered how to be anything else.

Avery didn't realize it, not as such, but he was becoming a more flexible person, one tiny bend at a time. And if some of those bends felt like breaking, well, any willow-whip could have told him something about what it was to yield.

The cave, which had been dim in the beginning, was growing steadily lighter as their group walked, going from pearl-tinted twilight to something much closer to the rosy light of dawn, as if somewhere in the distance, the sun was giving sincere thought to the act of rising. They walked on, and dawn broke into sunrise, buttery light suddenly filling the air, illuminating every dancing mote of dust, which rose up with their footsteps, chalk and sand and the crushed shells of long-dead marine creatures learning, however briefly, how to fly under their own precious power.

Zib laughed, and sped up, arrowing her footsteps toward a wide archway cut out of the cave wall. The others followed her, the Crow Girl bursting once more into birds in her hurry to see what was on the other side, until they all emerged into the bright, warm light of a seaside morning. They were standing on a beach that glittered like the sugar on a Christmas cookie, all pristine white and stretching out to the horizon both to the left and to the right, but yielding straight ahead to the lapping waves of an endless indigo sea. The water looked warm and gentle, and when it struck the sand it seemed to whisper, *Yes, children, good, children, yes, good children to come into me, come swim, come swim, come swim with the sirens and the sea fairies and all the good things that water can coddle and claim. Come, children, come.*

"Do you hear that?" asked Avery, suddenly nervous as he inched closer to Zib. She might be loud and wild and unaware of the importance of well-shined shoes, but she was from the same ordinary town as he was, and she knew that the ocean wasn't supposed to talk. Not so clearly, anyway, and not with such a bright and blazing need as this one.

"It wants us to go swimming," she said, voice dreamy. Then she shook her head and shot him a quick, alarmed look. "How does it want anything? It's the ocean. Oceans aren't supposed to want things."

"This is the Saltwise Sea," said Niamh. "This is where the King of Coins and the King of Cups collide. It's the truest border between their two domains."

"How does that make it so the water can talk?" asked Avery. "Water isn't supposed to talk."

"The King of Cups has the Page of Frozen Waters now, but he used to have the Lady of Salt and Sorrow," said Niamh. "She's the patron of my city. Everyone there loves her so, and she loves us, even if she can't pull herself out of the sea to talk to us any longer. We all know the Page is responsible for her losing her crown and her own good skin, but we can't prove it, because we can't find her bones."

"Has anyone told the King?" asked Zib.

The Crow Girl swirled back into being in front of them, pulling birds back into her body until she was only one thing, instead of many. "He doesn't care," she said, and there was more mourning in her voice than there usually was. "He has the Page, and she doesn't question what he wants or tell him not to do the terrible things he thinks will be pleasant. Maybe they are pleasant, for him. I don't know. I'm just a Crow Girl, I don't even have a name, and names change everything."

"The King of Cups is not your friend," said Niamh. "The King of Coins might be, because he believes everyone should be free to make up their own minds, even if that sometimes means they make up their minds to stand against him, and the Queen of Wands will be, if we can find where she's been taken and bring her back to the people who love her, but the King of Cups is not your friend. You have to remember that, if we're going to walk along the seaside."

"Do we have to?" asked Avery.

"Do you see anyplace else for us to go?"

"We could climb the cliff," said Avery, and gestured to the high rock wall behind them. The group turned and silently regarded it.

It was high and sheer, which are excellent qualities in a wall, if not so much in a path. Zib, who was the best climber among them, looked unsure.

"I could probably find a way up, if I had to," she said. "But it would be real easy to fall. And this sand is soft, but if you fell from far enough up, it would still be hard enough to break bones. I don't think we should climb up here. We can find another place, maybe, where the cliffs are shorter, or where they've broken on their own and made a path for us to follow. That would be better."

Avery, who had never known Zib to be anything other than pointlessly brave, gave her a betrayed look. She shook her head.

"I'm sorry," she said. "This is a very good adventure, but it's really happening. This isn't a story or a dream. We can get hurt here. If you fell off that cliff, you'd be well and truly hurt. All the way down to the bottom of you. None of us can put you back together, and I'm not ready to lose you."

Avery frowned but, never having had someone who would worry about losing him before, apart from his parents, couldn't argue with her. Instead, he shook his head, and said, "I think we should stay out of the water. I don't think we want to meet this Lady, not when she doesn't have a body anymore."

"She didn't give it up willingly," said Niamh. "I'd be safe, because something that's been drowned is hard to take apart, but she could have you out of your body like a hermit crab out of its shell if she wanted to, and we'd never be able to put you back in again."

Avery looked at her and shuddered, because he could see from the set of her chin and the seriousness in her eyes that she meant exactly what she was saying. He didn't want to be a hermit crab, in its shell or out of it. He wanted to be Avery, exactly Avery, whatever that meant.

"So we stay out of the water," said Zib. "We haven't lost each other, but we *have* lost the improbable road. Does it reach all the way to the seashore?"

The Crow Girl nodded with such enthusiasm that for a moment, it looked like she was going to nod her head clean off her shoulders. Which might have been possible, since her body was made entirely of individual birds, but would have been upsetting if it had happened. "The improbable road runs everywhere through the Up-and-Under," she said. "It can find you no matter where you are, if it wants to, and if you're doing things improbably enough."

Zib was starting to have serious concerns about how many of the things in the Up-and-Under seemed to be awake and aware and able to make their own decisions. She pushed them aside and spun in a circle, holding one arm stiffly out from her body. When she came to a stop, she was pointing to the east, down the beach. "We go *this* way," she said, as if spinning like a top were the absolutely most reasonable way of choosing a direction.

The others nodded, and as a group, the four of them moved down the beach, caught between the cliffside and the sea. Zib and Avery walked side by side, their hands occasionally brushing against each other, as if they had magnets in their palms that wanted only to be together but couldn't quite bridge the gap between them. Niamh cast longing glances at the water as they walked, but kept her distance from it, recognizing the wisdom of leaving the Lady to rest. The Crow Girl trotted alongside the rest, remaining on two legs, looking utterly content.

They didn't know how long they walked, for there was no real means of measuring time along the seaside; the tides shifted, but as none of them knew how to chart them, it made little difference, and the sun hung on the other side of the cliffs, out of sight and hence unhelpful. They walked long enough that their legs began to burn with the effort of walking on sand, and their throats grew dry, forgetting the taste of well water.

When the first flickers of green appeared ahead of them, they could all be forgiven for thinking they were seeing a mirage, something that wasn't really there and didn't deserve their attention. But as they continued to walk, the green grew clearer, and more difficult to deny. Zib grabbed Avery's hand, squeezing firmly.

"Do you see . . . ?" she asked, in a hushed tone.

"I do," he said.

They walked faster, striding across the beach until the sand under their feet changed into hard-packed earth, and they were stepping onto a little swath of ordinary soil, decorated with weeds and brambles and a small cluster of deeply welcome bonberry bushes, their bright pink fruit an almost irresistible enticement. There was a cottage near-buried amidst the green, with thick stone walls and one open, inviting window.

Avery approached the cottage cautiously, scarcely aware that he had lost Zib, who was filling her hands and mouth and stomach with small pink bonberries. "Hello?" he called, leaning up onto his toes to peer through the window. Inside the cottage was simple and clean, with a large bed that was a thousand times more inviting than the window had been. The pillows were crisp and plump and seemed to want nothing more than a boy to rest his head on them. "Is anyone home?"

There was dust on the table. He could see it from

outside. Whoever lived here was either a terrible housekeeper, or hadn't been home in quite some time. Carefully, he moved toward the cottage door. It had no knob, only a simple handle, which moved easily when he pushed it down. The door swung open. The air inside the cabin was sweet and dry.

Convinced that he was going to be caught at any moment, Avery stepped inside.

The first thing to catch his eye was the pump on the wall, which hadn't been visible when peering through the window. Avery moved toward it, and gave it an experimental shake. Water poured out into the basin, too quick for him to catch. Before he pumped again, he grabbed a cup from the counter and placed it under the spout. This time, the water went into the waiting vessel, and he laughed as he raised it to his lips.

It was even sweeter than the water from the well.

Behind him, the others were creeping into the cabin. Zib made a sound of wordless delight, followed by a thumping sound, as if someone had dropped a sack of potatoes on the floor. By the time Avery turned around, she was facedown on the bed, arms and legs sprawled out like a starfish. The Crow Girl was standing nearby, studying the contents of a low bookshelf with avian fixation, while Niamh stood by the door.

"You can rest," she said. "I don't need to sleep the same way you do. I don't get tired the way a breathing person does. So you can rest, if that's what you need."

Avery nodded slowly, finishing the water and setting the empty cup down on the edge of the basin. "You won't go looking for the improbable road without us?" he asked.

"No. I know you need to find the Queen of Wands if you want to go home, and I'm not going to run off and risk losing you."

"All right," said Avery. His legs felt very heavy as he walked across the room to Zib. Anyone who has ever gone on a long hike can tell you, truly, that they've never been so tired as when they were almost to the ending. His body knew that the ending was in sight, and was ready to stop moving. "Zib. Hey, Zib. Hey, move over, just a little, will you?"

Zib would not. She remained exactly as she was, face buried in the mattress, limbs akimbo. He leaned closer. It sounded as if she had started snoring faintly, already asleep.

Well. If she wanted to sleep so as to take up as much of the bed as physically possible, that was her problem, not his. Avery leaned over and grabbed her left arm, carefully moving it toward her body. She was asleep enough that when he let go, it stayed where he had placed it. That was encouraging. He repeated the process with her left leg, opening a slice of the mattress for his own use. Finally, he crawled into the bed next to her.

One good thing about not having shoes anymore: he didn't need to worry about taking his shoes off before he got in bed. Avery stretched his hands up over his head and his toes down toward the opposite wall, yawning a yawn so big that it cracked his jaw. Then he closed his eyes, rolling over so that his nose was buried in the rumpled curls of Zib's hair, and let sleep carry him off and away.

FOUR

POETRY AND PIRATES

Many things in the Up-and-Under were different from the things Avery and Zib had known in the ordinary town where they were born. It would be a lie to claim otherwise, and it is the job of a narrator to tell as few lies as possible, since the people who listen to us will always assume that we have been telling the truth. It is a mean trick for someone whose job it is to honestly account an adventure such as this one to exhibit an unnecessary disregard for the truth when there is no way to verify what's being said. So I am breaking the veil of the anonymous for a moment to address you, the reader, directly, and make this promise to you:

No matter how strange or improbable the things Avery, Zib, and their friends encounter on their journey through the Up-and-Under, I am telling you the truth as it was seen on those hazy, not-so-long-gone days. There may sometimes be other layers to the truth, things concealed beneath the superficial surface, but I will not say a thing was so if it was not, nor will I tell you a thing was not so when it was. You can trust me on this journey, even as Avery and Zib could trust the improbable road.

It was not long after Avery followed Zib into slumber that the Crow Girl burst into birds once more, flying out the window and finding roosts for herself in the briars and branches of the garden. She filled her many bellies with bonberries, until her beaks and talons dripped with pink juice. And then she closed her many eyes and slept, although it cannot be said whether she dreamt, for the dreams of birds are strange, tangled things, not recognizable as the dreams of children. The Crow Girl was, in that moment, still very close to being lost forever, for all that she was no longer in the cold hands of the King of Cups.

Inside the cottage, Niamh sat in a chair with a clear view of the door, being a silent, steady presence as the others slept. She would rest in her own way when the need came upon her, but the need was not upon her yet, and so she watched with open eyes, waiting to see whether the cottage's owner would appear and object to their uninvited guests.

The sun sank below the long edge of the sea, having put in an appearance over the high wall of the cliffs, and was gone. Darkness followed, first painting the horizon in pinks and oranges, then tucking all the colors away under a veil of indigo-black night. Stars glittered in the high, clear air, and it was good that Avery was asleep, for not a one of them would have been familiar to him, a stargazing boy who enjoyed evenings in the backyard with his book of constellations and his wide-eyed hunger for the universe. Their strangeness would have been yet another offense heaped on his narrow young shoulders, and he was near enough to the breaking point that he needed no more weight.

Zib wouldn't have noticed the strangeness of the stars, but she would have known something was wrong when she saw the moons, both of them too small and too dark to be the moon she knew, and most of all, each one cleaving close to the other, twins dancing through the darkened sky, and not a Man in the Moon standing elegant and alone. They would discover the sky soon enough, and inevitably; while there are many oddities that can be concealed from the eyes of curious children, an entire sky is not among them. But for the moment, they slept peacefully, too exhausted even to dream.

And Niamh waited.

The fog rolled in just before dawn, thick and white and heavy as a cotton blanket. It rolled across the garden, chilling the crows that roosted there, until each of them puffed out their feathers, one after the other, becoming black berries with the beaks of birds. The fog rolled on, coming through the open cottage window and filling the room with swirling, skirling whiteness. Niamh relaxed in her chair, closing her eyes and breathing deeply. They had fogs like this in the city she had come from, the city she had lost when the ice closed above it and trapped her alone in the vast dry world. Drowned girls didn't fare well in the endless dry, and she sometimes felt like she might crumble into dust and blow away in the next inquisitive wind.

But this fog—ah! This fog came with a feeling of infinite coolness—not damp, exactly, but not dry either. It wrapped around her, soothing away the aches and pains she had almost grown insensitive to, they had been there for so long. Niamh sighed, content.

Niamh had not considered how much human children liked to be warm and dry, or that Avery and Zib, although fully clothed, had fallen asleep atop the blankets and not moved all through the night, guzzling sleep like it was water and they had been lost in the desert for too long to remember moderation. Zib sat up in the bed, scrubbing at her face with one hand, eyes still scrunched shut.

"Is it morning?" she asked. If she had been older, Niamh would have thought she sounded drunk, like she'd toppled into bed after one too many cups of wine. Because she was still a child, she sounded more like she'd run face first into a wall and had yet to recover from the impact.

"No," said Niamh. "No, it's not morning. Go back to sleep."

Zib yawned, mouth opening so wide that her jaw cracked, finishing the figure Avery had begun when he yawned on his way into bed. She rubbed at her gummy eyes with the heels of her hands, and finally forced her eyelids open, squinting into the foggy white around her. She blinked, once, twice, a third time, and finally, in a voice that dripped with the early threads of panic, asked, "Niamh? Why is everything white?"

"The fog has rolled off the sea," said Niamh. "It's perfectly normal."

She was lying, of course, although not as badly as she could have been. Fog from the sea *was* perfectly normal, and she had seen it enough times to sound confident in her falsehood. Fog this thick, moving this far inland, was far from normal. It was unusual, and would have frightened Zib, who had never seen the fog swirl through the drowned places. If Zib became frightened, she would wake Avery, and Avery was more aggressive in his fear; he would splash it around like it was a wonderful gift that needed to be given as freely as possible. Niamh didn't want to be afraid right now. She wanted to watch the fog as it danced around her, and dream about the things it could contain.

"Oh," said Zib. She slid out of the bed, only wincing a little as her feet hit the cold cottage floor, and crept through the fog toward the window, peering out it at the whitewashed world. She could see no details through the fog, not even the crow-speckled garden. It was misty white, as far as her eyes could see.

"It's not safe to go outside right now," said Niamh. "You could walk right into the sea and never realize it."

"When will the fog lift?" asked Zib. She felt around until she found the pump Avery had used the night before. She couldn't find the cup, so she simply stuck her head beneath it and opened her mouth, pumping freezing water over her face. She came up sputtering and licking her lips, enough water in her mouth to make her tongue feel less like a strip of cotton wool.

"The sun should burn it away in a few hours."

"Oh," said Zib. "Good." Her stomach rumbled. She pressed a hand over it and looked longingly at the window. "I can't even go out into the garden?"

"There are brambles in the garden. If you tripped and fell into them, I wouldn't be able to come and help you get untangled. You could hurt yourself very badly."

"But the Crow Girl is out there."

"No, the murder of crows is out there. She came apart before she went to sleep, and they're not going to fly around while they can't see. Crows are clever that way, even if they're not smart the way you or I would measure smartness. She'll stay in pieces, in the trees, until it's safe for her to fly. Once it's safe, you can go picking bonberries."

Zib frowned a little, almost asking how Niamh, who had not traveled with them from the Forest of

Borders, wound up in charge. She swallowed the words like the poisoned pills they were. Niamh was in charge right now because she knew what the fog was, and how to survive dealing with it. Whoever knew the most was in charge, and that was how it had been since they entered the Up-and-Under, and that was the way things needed to continue if they wanted to have any chance of finding the Queen of Wands and getting home.

Zib had never been a particularly biddable child. Family stories aside, her first word hadn't been "why?"—it had been "no," which was almost as accurate to her personality—and she had never been terribly interested in following rules that weren't thoroughly and accurately explained. She wasn't stubborn or willful so much as she was simply curious. Adults seemed to understand everything, or at least spoke as if they did. She wanted to understand everything too. One of the things she had managed to understand so far was that it was best to let the person who understood the most be in charge, as long as they were willing to stop being in charge as soon as they weren't the most knowledgeable anymore.

With nowhere to go and nothing to do, Zib walked back to the bed and sat down on the edge, careful to give Avery as much space as she could. She was only just starting to realize that they'd shared the same bed. Her cheeks flushed pink at the thought of what her father would say if he knew that she'd been sleeping with a boy, even if she hadn't changed into her pajamas, even if she didn't remember anything other than the sleep itself. She sometimes thought that when her father blustered about boys, he was using words she knew—like "sleep" and "play"—to mean something she'd never heard before and didn't want to understand.

Avery was still out cold. That made sense, Zib reasoned; she'd known almost as soon as she met him that he wasn't the sort of person who saw a tree and started trying to figure out how to climb it, or who saw a field and wondered how long it would take to run across it. If the last few days had exhausted *her*, they would have done even worse to *him*. Avery was delicate. He would wake up when he was ready.

If Zib had been a little older, she might have understood what her father was afraid of, and more, she might have felt jealousy at the idea that Avery was somehow delicate enough to need more time and attention and a softer bed than she did. If she'd been a little older, she might have started seizing on the adult ideas of equality, which is almost never equal at all, because it pretends that if everyone is given exactly the same amount of everything, the world will somehow twist inward on itself and turn fair. Giving Avery the entire bed because he was delicate would have been unfair to Zib, who was just as tired and sore. But giving it to her because she was a girl would have been unfair to Avery, and giving it to Niamh because she was older would have been unfair to all of them. They were not, and would never be, all entirely the same. It was unreasonable to ask them to be. Zib yawned and got up for more water, wondering how it was that children seemed to understand what fairness looked like, but lost that understanding as they grew up, wearing it away like the shine on a pair of polished shoes.

The fog inside the cottage was getting thinner; she was able to find the cup this time, rather than needing to stick her head entirely under the spigot. She pumped twice to fill it with cold, clear water, and drank deeply before refilling the cup and offering it to Niamh. "Did you want some?"

"Thank you," said Niamh politely, and took the cup, and dumped it out over her head, dousing herself. She was always damp, had been damp before pouring water on herself, but for one shining moment, she was actually *wet*. Then her hair and skin seemed to drink the water down, and it vanished, leaving her looking as if she'd gone for a swim in the sea about an hour before, and was now well on her way to full dryness.

It would have been unsettling, once, for the Zib who had existed before she'd seen a girl break into birds, before she'd felt the feathers splintering off from her own bones and struggling to break through the skin. Now, a girl who drank with her entire body seemed only reasonable. Zib reclaimed the cup and carried it back to the sink. They might be trespassing on someone else's property, but they could at least be polite while they were breaking and entering.

Outside the window, the faint outlines of the

cliff and the trees in the garden were returning; it no longer seemed quite as possible to get lost in the fog and fall into the sea. Zib gave Niamh a hopeful look. Niamh nodded, and was still in the process of nodding when Zib shot out the door like a conker flung by a slingshot, moving so fast that it was a wonder her feet didn't get tied together and send her sprawling.

The ground outside was much colder than the floor of the cottage. Zib, motivated by both hunger and her innate fear of confinement—a fear that had only grown worse after the Page of Frozen Waters had flung her into a cage—barely noticed. She plunged into the fog, pursuing the hulking shape of what she assumed was a bonberry bush, and stopped only when her fingers brushed foliage. She closed her eyes, correctly assuming that having no sight would be less confusing than having blurred, irregular sight, letting her fingers skirt through the leaves until they found the round, reassuring bodies of the bonberries.

One by one, she plucked them and popped them into her mouth, letting them burst into sweetness that coated her throat and tongue before trickling deliciously down to fill her stomach. A weight settled on her left shoulder. She offered the next bonberry she plucked to the crow that had landed there, and smiled again when the fruit was taken from her fingers. Steadily, she ate and ate as more crows landed on her head and arms, and when one of them rasped a bright morning caw, she opened her eyes and beheld the garden.

The fog was still there, hanging thick and cottony

among the brambles and branches, but it had pulled back enough that she could see the flowers on their stems and the cobwebs glittering with morning dew. The garden had returned as the sunlight pouring down from above in great, buttery shafts came to burn the fog away. There was so much fog in the air that everything was still dim and gray, like it was twilight rather than morning.

More and more crows were beginning to stir. Zib looked at the one that had come to her first, seated on her shoulder with its beak still sticky with bonberry juice.

"I would like it if we could have a conversation, and if you could help me pick berries to take inside for Avery and Niamh," she said. "Crows are wonderful, but you're not so good for talking to, unless I want to really be talking to myself."

The crow cocked its head, regarding her for a moment before it made a small croaking sound and flung itself into the air. Zib had never seen birds that took flight the way the Crow Girl did. She flew as if she was attacking the sky and expected to be repelled at any moment by the creatures that actually belonged there. All across the garden, crows took wing, crashing toward each other and finally colliding a few feet away from Zib in a great cacophony of wings and feathers that consolidated into the shape of one skinny teenage girl in a black feather dress.

"Are there other things like you?" blurted Zib. It was a rude question, but she wasn't sorry to have asked it. It felt like the sort of thing that needed to be answered, either now or in the future, and she was growing increasingly tired of pushing things into the future rather than handling them in the aching, immediate now.

"You saw the rest of the flock when the King tried to take you," said the Crow Girl.

"No, I mean, I know there are other crows, but are there *other* things?" Zib frowned earnestly, her hands busying themselves with the picking of ripe pink berries. "Are there boys who are also knots of toads, or girls who are a camp of bats when they don't feel like walking on two legs? I know you traded your name for feathers. Can people trade for other things?"

"Ah," said the Crow Girl, and "Oh," said the Crow Girl, and "Yes, and no," said the Crow Girl. She began her own berry-picking, clever fingers clearing branches in seconds as she pulled the fruit into her palms. She kept her eye on the bush, not looking at Zib. "That was where I had the idea, you see. There was a boy, when I was younger, and he could become a whole shoal of salmon when he didn't want to think like a boy did, when he wanted to swim freely and be left alone. I had the idea that maybe I could be like him, if I tried hard enough. That I could have freedom when I wanted it, and a cage when I wanted that instead. So I went looking. I slipped away from the people who were meant to keep watch over me, and their faces went with my name, so now I don't even know who I left behind."

Zib gazed at her for a moment before plucking a last few berries and turning toward the cottage. "Avery should be awake by now," she said. "He'll be hungry. We didn't eat much last night. Do you think flavor fruit trees will grow this close to the water?"

"I think this is where Coins meet Cups, and the Queen of Wands created the flavor fruit," said the Crow Girl, sounding relieved by the change of subject. "Her magic doesn't work well here, where two forces oppose her. Wands center on fire, creating and destroying both. Coins stand for earth, and Cups for water. I think it's bonberries and whatever comes out of the sea for as long as we're here."

Zib turned back to her, mouth curving upward in the beginning of a laugh, and froze at the sight of a silhouette behind the fog. It was tall and elegant, and she knew it at once, for all that she had never in her life been this close to a seashore. "A ship!" she cried. "A ship, a ship!"

She whirled then, and ran into the cottage, her hands full of berries and pink stains around her mouth. The Crow Girl ran after her.

Inside, Avery was still sleeping soundly. Zib dropped the berries onto the mattress next to his head and gave him a hearty shake. "There's a ship coming!" she shouted. "It's sailing out of the fog! Eat fast, it must be the owner!"

Her reasoning was easy to follow, for all that it would be strange to see a man walking down a street and assume that he owned every house around him.

There was only this one cottage along the long sweep of the beach, and it was well-tended enough that it clearly belonged to someone. Now there was a single ship coming toward the shore, willing to risk the dangers posed by the fog, and it was reasonable to guess that it belonged either to the cottage's owner, or to someone who had reason to wish them ill.

Avery opened his eyes, squinting blearily at Zib for a moment before he sat up and began gathering berries off the bedcovers. He squashed a few of them in the process, and would have felt worse about it had Zib not so clearly been worked up and worried, moving to pull Niamh from her seat and hurry her toward the door. They nearly collided with the Crow Girl in the doorway, the three of them becoming a brief, unscheduled slapstick show as the Crow Girl tried not to drop the berries she had gathered, and Niamh tried not to trip and fall.

Avery got out of the bed, hands full of berries, and cast one longing look toward the sink before joining the others at the door.

"Hurry, hurry, hurry!" chanted Zib, single-minded in her need to get them outside before the ship in the fog could dock and its occupant could make their way to the cottage. She was moving faster than circumstances warranted, but Zib had never been one to take things slow, not even when it might have been the better choice for the situation.

The Crow Girl took a step back, allowing Zib to push Niamh outside. Zib took her hands off the drowned girl's shoulders, and Niamh took a deep breath, pushing her damp hair out of her eyes. "What happened?" she asked, looking from Zib to the Crow Girl.

The Crow Girl took a deep breath as she solemnly poured the berries in her hands into Niamh's. "There's a ship," she said portentously. "Sailing through the fog toward us. Zib thinks it's the owner of this cottage, and they might not like us being here when they land."

Zib nodded, so vigorously that her hair wound up in her mouth, and she had to spit it out and cough a little before she said, "People don't like trespassers much. I went into the backyard of my next-door neighbor once, and she threw a *brick* at me! All I did was eat a couple of her tomatoes!"

Niamh, whose hands were sticky with berry juice, nodded more slowly. "Then we should probably get back to the beach. Avery?"

"I'm right here," said Avery, nudging Zib outside so that he could pull the door shut behind himself. For a moment, the four of them stood motionless in the garden, two with hands full of berries, two with berry stains on their lips and fingers. Then, as one, they started moving, back toward the endless sweep of sand.

The outline of the ship was clearer now, like a cutout in the fog, which had continued to thin and waft away as the sunlight tore at its substance. The edge of the beach was obscured by the fog; it was impossible in that moment to tell how far from land the ship actually was. Still, they hurried down to the beach, Avery and Niamh eating out of their hands like horses as they walked, until the berries were gone, and only faint pink stains remained.

"I wish there had been time to get some water," remarked Avery. "I'm thirsty as anything."

"You can drink from the sea," said Niamh.

"Saltwater only makes people thirstier," said Avery.

Niamh blinked. "Ah, but this is the *Saltwise* Sea," she said, as if that statement made all the sense in the world. "If you ask it to move the salt aside for you, it will. Don't oceans work that way where you come from?"

"Wished-for wells, help-kelp, and now a Saltwise Sea," said Avery, crossness washing away the last of his exhaustion. "Is there *anything* in the Up-and-Under that doesn't speak English?"

"What's English?" asked the Crow Girl.

Avery turned to blink at her, too stunned to speak for a long moment. When he finally found his voice, it was to say, "The language we're all using. It's called English."

"No, it's not," said Niamh. "Why would we speak a language called 'English' here? Who are the Eng? Where is their country?"

"Uh," said Avery. "The English people live in a country called 'England.' Zib and I live in a country called 'America.' It was colonized by the English a whole bunch of years ago, and they left their language behind when they left."

"Why did they leave?" asked the Crow Girl.

"We got tired of them being in charge of us, and so we fought a war against them," said Avery. "That's what people do, when they don't want to be colonized anymore. They fight wars, and if they win them, they get to become their own country."

"But are you really your own country if you're still speaking English, even after the people who taught it to you are gone?" asked Niamh. "Weren't there people in your country before it was colonized? Did they speak American? Why didn't you go and learn American from them after the English left?"

"Um," said Avery, suddenly uncomfortable. "I think because the English killed them all in order to take their land away."

"Oh," said the Crow Girl, "You speak the language of murder. No wonder I like you so much!"

"Here in the Up-and-Under, we speak the language of whoever holds the Impossible City," said Niamh. "Right now, that means we all speak Wandish. You've been speaking Wandish since you got here. If someone else seizes the City, the language will change."

"It sounds like English to me," said Zib. "It's sounded like English the whole time. How will we know if the language changes?"

"I never learned Coinage," said Niamh. "Earth and Water are not friends, although we can form borders together, and sometimes mud. Mud is a friend. It's complicated."

"This is all very confusing," said Avery.

"Look," said Zib. "There's a rowboat."

They all turned and looked, and indeed, there was a small boat rowing from the larger ship toward the shore. The ship had stopped some distance away, anchoring itself in both the sea and the fog. There only seemed to be one person doing the rowing. For all that they had the newcomer solidly outnumbered, the four children took a big step backward, away from the tideline, toward the solid, patient cliffs.

"Ahoy!" called an unfamiliar voice. The rowboat stopped moving, with a little bump that implied it had reached solid ground and was done with its purpose. The rower dropped the oars and stood, stepping out of the boat.

As they didn't immediately sink into the water, they had definitely reached land.

The Crow Girl trembled without bursting into birds, and Zib reached over to squeeze her wrist, which was the only reward that could currently be given for her bravery and forbearance. The Crow Girl shot her a grateful look. Instincts could be difficult things to fight, and the instinct that told her to be birds was very strong. Niamh shifted slightly, squaring her posture so that she was looking directly toward the approaching stranger, her body between them and the children.

Avery moved a few inches closer to Zib. He didn't think of himself as particularly brave, and thought he might never begin to, but he could be braver when he was with her. She made it feel almost easy. So he stood by her side, and waited for the stranger to come.

Through the mist, through the fog, one step at a time, until the man was standing right in front of the foursome. He was young, although older than any of the four of them, too young to be a king, too young to be a father, but easily old enough to be a sailor. He was dressed simply, for the sea, in a white linen shirt, black trousers, boots that Zib envied instantly, and a belt that wrapped three times around his hips before it stopped. He had no hat, and no jewelry, but a wide, honest face that seemed too new for the rest of him. His eyes were the color of the help-kelp from the cave, and his hair was long and tangled. He put a hand on the hilt of the knife at his belt, blinking at the children.

"What are you doing here?" he asked. "The King of Coins closed all paths to the sea a year ago, and we've seen no strangers since."

"Not all paths," said Niamh. "He owns the land but not the water. We had a helping hand from some of the kelp. It thought we needed to be here."

"My captain will be glad to know that it's possible to come and go if you can breathe water," said the man. His eyes narrowed. "Wait. Not all of you look like you can breathe water."

"You can recognize a drowned girl, but not a Crow Girl?" asked the Crow Girl. "Shame. Shame on your education and your ideals. Shame on everything you love."

The man frowned. "We don't have Crow Girls this far to the west. We don't have people made of animals at all. The King of Cups forbids them."

"The King of Cups made me," said the Crow Girl, and took a single stiff-legged step toward the man. "I was a girl once. Just a girl, not a murder, and I had a name and knew it, could show it and share it with people when I wanted to. He took that away when he turned me into what I am now, and he did it with my permission, because somehow the idea of wings was better than the idea of standing still. So don't tell me he forbids the birds to fly. The birds will always fly."

"I tell you what I know," said the man. "So. A drowned girl and a beauty of beasts, and . . . what? What are you?" He turned his attention on Avery and Zib. "How did you come to be here, and why are you so close to my captain's cottage?"

"We're here because the help-kelp pulled us through a wished-for well," said Avery. "Nothing in this place makes sense. We're from America. We're not from here at all."

"We're not birds, and we haven't drowned," said Zib. "We're children."

"Children," said the man, in a tone that spoke of disbelief and wonder at the same time, as if there were no contradiction between them. "*Human* children?"

It occurred belatedly to Avery that while they had met people who *looked* very human, none of them technically had been, or if they had once, they weren't anymore—Niamh was very clear that she was a drowned girl, not a human child, and it was difficult to say what the Crow Girl really was. He swallowed, moving closer still to Zib, and said, "Yes, sir. Human children. We climbed over a wall into the Forest of Borders."

"We've been following the improbable road," said Zib. "We're on a quest."

"Is that so?" asked the man. He shifted positions, gesturing back toward his rowboat. "The improbable road goes where it likes in the Up-and-Under. That's part of what makes it so difficult to define. Perhaps now, it leads you to my lady's ship. I know she would like to meet the human children who have so enjoyed her hospitality."

Avery's cheeks colored red as Zib scuffed her toe against the sand. "Maybe we should," he said. "It would be the polite thing to do."

Niamh cleared her throat. "We travel together or not at all," she said. "These are my friends. I'll not have you hurting them because they picked a few berries and drank some water."

"All of us," said the Crow Girl.

The man nodded slowly. "All of you. Of course. But we have no cisterns or carrion-heaps on the ship. There would be nowhere to your standards for you to sleep."

"Drowned girls don't sleep, and we certainly don't spend our time in cisterns," said Niamh.

"I . . . I can stay together to be with my friends," said the Crow Girl. "If I'm always a girl, I don't need any carrion. Thank you for offering. I do appreciate it."

"If we come with you, will you bring us back to shore when we ask?" Zib asked the question earnestly, eyes wide and bright. She was still learning the art of being afraid of strangers. "We need to find our way back to the improbable road eventually, so we can't go off and be on your ship forever."

"Of course," said the man.

Zib, who had also not yet learned the art of listening for lies, believed him at once. She nodded happily as she turned back to the others. "We should go," she said. "We can't keep using the cottage without permission, and we can't get permission without going to the ship. We can see more of the shoreline from the ship, so we could scout out our way, and then come back to the shore and keep going."

Avery nodded as well, more reluctantly. "We can ask his captain if she knows a way over the cliff and back to dryer land."

"Then we go," said the Crow Girl brightly. The sailor looked at her with darkness in his eyes, and said nothing, only motioned toward the waiting shape of his rowboat.

The children followed him as he walked, forming a ragged line with Avery and Zib at the front, walking, as they so often did, side by side. The Crow Girl followed them, feet sinking into the sand and leaving prints that barely looked human, and Niamh followed *her*, leaving a trail of shining dampness behind her, like the slime of a slug.

One by one, they climbed into the rowboat, and when Niamh was seated, the sailor followed her, pushing off from the shore and beginning the long, slow row toward the waiting shape of the ship in the fog.

FIVE

GETTING SOMEWHERE

The rowboat moved more slowly with the weight of five passengers than it had with the weight of one. It became quickly clear that the sailor was struggling. Niamh leaned over the side and trailed the fingers of her right hand in the water. Almost immediately, a low wave surged up behind them, pushing them forward, toward the ship. The sailor brightened, as if this change in the water had taken most of the struggle from his shoulders, and continued to row. The water grew higher, pushing them faster, until the wake behind them looked much like the wake from an outboard motor.

The sailor pulled his oars inside the boat, lest they be lost, while Niamh kept her fingers in the water.

Avery shot her a look of frank surprise. "Are you doing this?" he asked.

"I am," she confirmed.

"How? And why?"

"Why, because it seemed cruel to make our host struggle when I had a way to speed things along," said Niamh. "How, because my city isn't far from here, as the sardine swims, and the water knows every one of us by name. I can't go home, but that doesn't mean I've been forgotten. The ocean always remembers."

Avery threw his hands in the air as he slumped backward in the boat. "Is there *anything* in the Up-and-Under that doesn't have opinions about things?"

"Berries, usually," said the Crow Girl. "Daisies. Oh, and slugs. Slugs don't have a lot of room in their bodies for brains, and so they don't tend to think much of anything. They don't like to be eaten, but I have to assume it's like that in your country as well. Nothing living likes to be consumed."

"But if the water can have opinions, how can we drink it?" asked Avery. "That's consuming! It makes us vampires!"

"What's a vampires?" asked the Crow Girl.

"People are mostly water, my mother says," said Zib. "We're water with opinions."

"The water never notices a glass or two," said Niamh, shooting a quelling glance at Zib. "Humans came from the sea, the same as everything else, and part of what it means to be water is movement. Water is transformation. It becomes fog, it becomes rain, it becomes the blood in a little boy's veins and the steam rising off a field in the sun. It becomes food. The transmutation of water is constant and undeniable, and water isn't water anymore when it stops. Drink your water, and don't worry about hurting its feelings. It wants to be transmuted."

Avery, who couldn't imagine a world where he would want to be transmuted by passing through the body of something other than himself, lowered his arms, leaned against the side of the boat, and said nothing.

Across from him, Zib leaned over the side of the boat and trailed her fingers in the water, washing the berry juice away. Spray hit her in the face and she laughed, throwing her head back in joy, hair whipping in the wind. She looked like some sort of wild wind-sprite that had settled long enough to enjoy a few minutes sheathed in skin, like she would burn away with the last of the fog, and for a moment, Avery was afraid. He didn't want Zib to disappear. He still wasn't entirely sure he *liked* her—she was nothing like the children his parents had encouraged him to spend time with, who had always been polished and polite and disinclined to run, screaming, toward the nearest danger. Zib was none of those things. If there was something that shouldn't be approached, Zib was probably already up to her knees in it, and covered in some new sort of sludge. So maybe they weren't *friends*, precisely, or at least not the kind of friends they would have been on the other side of the wall, but they were *bound* now, in some new kind of relation to each other.

Like eggs and flour put into the same cake, they made something between them that they could never have been on their own, something bigger and better than their solitude. Avery couldn't call that friendship. He still knew it was important, and that he didn't want it to end.

Zib pulled her hands back into the boat as they neared the side of the ship, glancing over at the Crow Girl, who had gone quite pale and a little green around the edges. "Are you all right?" she asked.

"Niamh knows she's water," said the Crow Girl. "She understands water, and water hasn't forsaken her. I don't know what I am."

"How do you not know what you are?" asked Zib.

"Crows are air," said the Crow Girl. "But humans can be anything. Four humans in a pack can belong to four different kingdoms, follow four different elements. I'm human as often as I'm crows. I don't know where I belong. I gave that up when I gave away my name. Whatever I am is half-air, because crows, and air and water are friends, but they're not the same thing. The part of me that's air is in a panic. It wants to fly away, because I shouldn't be surrounded by water and not able to stop myself from sinking."

"So you do know something," said Zib.

"I know a lot of things, but I don't know which of them is meant to be important right now, and if you know it you should tell me," said the Crow Girl.

"You know you're not water, or you'd feel safe right now, like you were supposed to be right where you are."

The Crow Girl brightened. "That's true! When I find the thing that doesn't make me feel like this, I'll know I've found the thing I belong to."

Niamh also pulled her hands out of the water, and the current that had been driving them forward died back into ordinary waves, leaving them to nestle gently against the side of the bigger ship, like a leaf bumping into the shore. The sailor at the oars looked relieved, cupping his hands around his mouth and shouting, "Permission to come aboard!" up at the waiting deck.

It didn't sound like a question. It didn't sound like a command. Zib frowned, looking to Avery for clarification. He shrugged. "Sometimes grownups say things that only matter because they have to be said," he said. "It's a ritual thing, that's what my father says. It's just doing what's supposed to be done."

"Huh," said Zib, as a rope ladder unfurled from the ship's edge, dropping down to land a few feet from the rowboat.

The sailor gestured to it grandly. "After you," he said.

Zib, who had never seen a challenge she didn't want to climb, was the first to move. She flung herself at the rope ladder with giddy abandon, grabbing hold of the rungs and swarming upward as nimbly as a lemur. The gentle sway and roll of the ship didn't appear to slow her in the slightest, and in a matter of seconds, she was at the top, climbing over the ship's rail to the deck.

Oh, but we cannot stay with her there, for all that things are happening, for we must get the others aboard. Down in the rowboat, Avery and the Crow Girl exchanged a queasy look, both all too aware that they lacked Zib's talents in this arena. Slowly, Avery moved toward the rope, leaned out, and grabbed hold of it, pulling himself up.

It was difficult. But the second rung was more so, as his arms and shoulders protested this ill treatment. He forced himself to keep climbing. It was the only way to reach the top. The ladder sagged and then stabilized as someone else hopped on; he looked back to see the Crow Girl pulling herself miserably along. If his arms were unaccustomed to supporting his weight, what must it be like for someone who normally flew away whenever things got difficult? Not many aspects of her bird bodies seemed to translate into her human one; all that flying had done nothing to make her arms stronger.

And why wasn't she flying away? She should have done it on instinct if nothing else, rather than struggling with the rest of them.

The sailor was the next to mount the rope ladder, after a brief argument with Niamh, who remained in the boat as she watched him climb away. Finally, last of them, she took hold of the bottom rung, and grimaced as the natural and integral dampness of her hands soaked it clean through, leaving it too slippery for anyone else to use.

The sailor and Niamh were better climbers than Avery and the Crow Girl, and quickly caught up with them. The sailor smirked a little as he tilted his head back and called to the top, "Reel us in!"

The ladder began to move, hauled over the rail by strong, practiced hands, pulling all four of its passengers along. Avery, who was halfway up, swallowed his protests. He didn't want to climb the rest of the way. His desire not to do that was stronger than the need to yell at the sailor for not telling him that they could be pulled before exhausting themselves.

He was the first of the three to reach the rail. He grabbed it, transferring his grip from rope to wood, and tumbled onto the deck, landing at the feet of the two men who were pulling in the ladder. They smirked down at him and kept hauling.

And now we will step back a bit, to when Zib first set foot on that same deck, that we might braid the two experiences together into a single strand of story, unbroken and unbreaking. She tumbled over the rail, unable to quite keep her grasp on the slick wood, and landed on her bottom with a solid thump. Zib was the veteran of a hundred tumbles, a thousand falls, and barely noticed the impact. She was too busy gazing at the woman who was waiting for her there, next to the mast.

The woman was tall, with broad hips and broad shoulders, and a waist that pinched inward to form an hourglass, no doubt helped by the black leather cincher she wore, which seemed to Zib to be something like a very broad belt that wound the woman in, compressing her into a reduced amount of space. It did no good, no good at all, for there was nothing that could have been done to make this woman seem small; she was designed and destined to occupy entire oceans. Her face was not what Zib had been taught to consider "beautiful," being sharp and cold instead of rounded and warm, but her eyes were the color of sunlight on the sea, and her hair was as gray as foam against the beach, falling in a froth to her waist, as wild and unconstrained as the rest of her. A black band that looked very much like the cincher kept the hair away from her face, which was probably safer, for when the ship was in motion, the wind would be high.

She wore a red vest and tight black trousers and impractical red boots, and Zib fell in love with her instantly. She scrambled to her feet, pushing her own tangled hair back with both hands.

"Who are you?" asked the woman.

"Hepzibah," said Zib. "But everyone calls me 'Zib.'"

"Still growing into your name," said the woman. "You can call me Captain Alas. This is my ship, the *Windchaser.* My word here is law. Do you understand, Zib?"

"Yes, ma'am," said Zib, and bowed shallowly, unsure of what else she should do. "I appreciate you letting us come on board."

"Don't make me regret it," said the captain, and then came the shout from below, and the rope was pulled to the deck, and the two stories reunited.

Avery fell over the rail with a loud thump and stayed motionless where he fell for several seconds, until one of the sailors grasped his arm and pulled him to his feet. The Crow Girl was next over the rail. She scrambled to her feet almost immediately, looking around with wide, terrified eyes. The feathers of her dress puffed out slightly, as if she was trying to make herself look bigger.

Niamh appeared next. She was the first one not to fall. The slick dampness of the wood didn't seem to trouble her in the slightest. She grasped it, slithered over, and stood tall and calm next to the anxious Crow Girl. Avery stared at her, unable to fathom how she could have passed the sailor on a narrow, damp ladder. She met the captain's eyes and nodded acknowledgment, but she didn't bow. Instead, she moved to the side to allow the sailor to dismount the ladder.

He did so gracefully, clearly long practiced at this particular arrival, and even balanced atop the rail for a moment before hopping down. "Captain!" he said, spreading his arms. "I found strangers on the beach!"

"Not so strange," said the captain, with a hint of amusement. "What were they doing there?"

"They broke into your cottage and were taking advantage of its luxuries," said the sailor.

Avery, who had never considered a single bed or

a working pump to be luxuries, startled slightly. The captain turned to look at him, her expression growing cool. "Is this so?" she asked.

"Um, uh, yes, ma'am," he said. "We didn't know it was your cabin, though. We just knew that it was late and we were cold and we needed a place to go. Um. Ma'am. We were careful. We didn't make a mess."

As he said that, he thought of the berry stains he'd left on her quilt, and it was all he could do not to wince.

"I understand what it is to be lost and to be cold," said the captain. "But trespassing is still a crime, and I would be a poor pirate captain if I allowed such an insult against myself to stand. The four of you violated my property, and so you will replace it."

"You want us to build you a whole new cottage?" asked the Crow Girl. "I don't know how to do that. I don't think any of us know how to do that. Or where we would get the wood, or the windows, or any of those things."

"No," said the captain, lips harboring the shadow of a smile. "You will *be* my property, to replace the sanctity you stole. For one week, you'll serve me on this ship and do whatever I command."

"Pardon, Captain, but your man said he would return us to the shore whenever we asked," said Niamh. "How will you reconcile making us your property and offering us no avenue of escape with the promises made by a member of your crew?"

"There's nothing to reconcile," said the captain

airily. "We *will* return you to the shore when you ask. If you ask now, you do it without paying your debts, and all the Saltwise Sea will know you for cheats and scoundrels. You're a drowned girl, aren't you? From the city of Sylphan, beneath the Unmelting Lake. The sea reaches that far, through tiny channels in the earth. It flows into the waters of your lake, and it will carry the message of your malfeasance to everyone you've left behind, everyone who wonders where you've gone and if you're ever coming home. Are you willing to do that to your family?"

Niamh's eyes darkened. She looked down, first at her own feet, and then away. The captain nodded. "I thought not," she said.

"I'm not from a city in a lake, and I don't care if people think I'm a thief," said the Crow Girl. "People already think crows are thieves, even when we don't steal anything at all. So it's no real matter to me."

"But it's a matter to your friends," said the captain. "Would you have people start to think that you stole them, instead of earning them fair and square, the way friendships are customarily acquired?"

The Crow Girl looked uncertain. The captain smiled.

"I am Captain Alas, and this is my ship," she said, to the new arrivals. "Here, my word is law, and you do not argue with me. For the next week, you are junior members of my crew, until you've worked off your debt for the use of my private, personal property. At the end of that week, we will return here, and you may go ashore if you so desire. You will not be harmed while you sail with us. You will be fed, and given a safe place to sleep, all four of you together, even"—and here her mouth pursed in disapproval—"the flock of crows. They'll be staying as they are now as long as they're onboard, of course, we can't have birds flapping all over a working pirate ship."

"Pirates?" gasped Avery, breaking out of the soothing spell her words had cast. "But if you're pirates, we can't sail with you! Pirates are cruel, wicked people, and we aren't cruel, or wicked, or thieves. If we stay, you'll make us all those things!"

"Maybe that's true of some pirates, but we're not pirates because we want to be cruel, or wicked, or thieves," said the captain. "We're pirates because the King of Cups refused us the sea. We sail against his command, which makes us outlaws at the very least, and when his ships attack us for the crime of sailing without his flag on our mast, we fight them off and, yes, raid their holds, as a form of payment for the damages they do us. If that makes us wicked, then wicked we must be, but all we ever intended to do was sail. The sea calls us all, and we had to answer, or be denying the will of something much greater and older than ourselves." The captain turned her face into the wind, and spoke the rest of her words in profile. "It does no good to deny the sea. She'll have what she wants in the end, however hard we try to deny her. The King of Cups thinks she can be trifled with, but some of us still fear death by water. We sail under her flag, not his."

Zib looked up at the mast, and indeed, the flag waving there was blue, only blue, solid blue from side to side. If ever the sea had designed a flag, it was this one. She looked back down again, focusing on Captain Alas.

"Why does the Crow Girl have to be a girl all the time while she's here? Why don't you like her?"

"The crows belong to the King of Cups," said the captain. "It's easy for a single crow to slip away and carry secrets to the King. I won't have that. I need to protect my crew."

"I don't serve the King of Cups!" protested the Crow Girl. "Well, not anymore, I mean. I ran away and he let me go."

The captain blinked quizzically as she turned to face the Crow Girl. "He . . . let you go?"

"He saw me going and he didn't pull me back. That feels like letting go to me."

The captain held her eyes for a long beat before she nodded. "Then you're welcome here, but I still need you to stay as you are. The ship will keep you in one piece, for your own safety. My sailors view crows as bad omens and spies for the King. They might react before they think."

The Crow Girl nodded, shrinking back on herself so that she was pressed up against the rail. The slightest touch would have sent her toppling over the side, toward the waiting, hungry sea.

For the first time, the captain smiled. It was a radiant expression; it made her harsh features somehow beautiful, in the way a mountain can be beautiful. It can still be dangerous, for it is still a mountain, and mountains are not forgiving to climbers simply because those climbers love them, and its body will still lie littered with their bones, but beauty and danger are not exclusive states. In that moment, she was lovely, and Avery fell a little bit in love with her.

Zib did not, for Zib had already fallen. She didn't need a mountain to be beautiful in order to love it. She only needed it to be a mountain, tall and deadly and waiting to be climbed.

"Then will you pay your debts?" asked the captain, in a mild, quizzical tone.

"We will," said Niamh.

"Excellent," said the captain. She snapped her fingers, and the sailor who had escorted them to the ship hurried to her side. "Jibson, find them a place to bunk down, and get them shoes."

"Shoes," said Avery, excited and relieved. "Really?"

"Shoes," whined Zib, disappointed. "Really?"

"Yes, really," said the captain, to both of them at once. "The deck is slippery and full of splinters. You'll need shoes to work properly without hurting yourselves. I aim to get a solid week's work out of you, and I'll not have you skiving off because you stubbed your toes on the mast."

"As you say, Captain," said Jibson. He spread his arms enough to let him gesture them forward, like he was trying to command a flock of sheep. The Crow Girl looked at him, blank-eyed with fear, and allowed herself to be herded. Avery and Zib shrugged and followed her, leaving Niamh to trail along behind. The captain stayed where she was, watching them all go.

SIX

IT'S ALWAYS THERE

The cabin our foursome would be sharing for the next week was located below the deck, tucked away in what seemed to be a largely unused section of the hold. It was near enough to the hull that they could hear the waves slapping against the side, as well as every creak, rustle, and groan of the wood itself. There would be no silent nights here, not surrounded as they were by the singing of the sea.

The cabin itself was small and square, with four bunks attached to its walls by carefully polished chains. The mattresses were spare and hard, each equipped with a single thin blanket and a pillow that was scarcely any thicker. There was a narrow wardrobe in which they were all expected to store whatever clothing they weren't wearing at any given moment; it would have been more of a problem had any of them possessed more than a single set of clothes. Jibson ushered them inside.

"Each of you pick a bunk," he said. "It doesn't matter which one, and don't fight. The captain doesn't like it when her sailors fight, and for right now, I suppose we're to treat you as sailors. Not proper sailors. Cabin boys, perhaps. We'll train you up until you earn the title!" He laughed, deep and hearty, like he had just said something deeply funny.

The children, clustered as they were in the center of the cabin, looked at him mistrustfully, and said nothing. Jibson sobered.

"Oh, come," he said. "You had to know you'd be called on to pay for what you took. Nothing's free when the King of Coins is involved."

"How many kings does one sea need?" asked Zib crossly. "The King of Cups means we can't trust the crows, but the King of Coins means we have to pay for sleeping in a bed that no one else was using and drinking a few cups of water, even though we didn't hurt anyone, and didn't take anything away from anybody else. I don't want any more kings. I'm done with kings."

"So are we!" said Jibson, for all appearances happily. "That's why we sail under the banner of the sea herself, for the ocean knows no kings, and the tide knows no queens, and those who pledge themselves to the sea need fear no crowns. I'm sorry if you feel I misled you, but if you'll let me get shoes on your feet, I can take you to the ship's mess for a proper meal."

Zib wanted to argue. As her stomach growled and prowled within her like a starving beast, she found she could do no such thing. Perhaps this would be a good thing after all. She had always wanted to see a real pirate ship, and now she could. They would be fed, and have a safe, warm place to sleep, and at the end of it all, they could return to the shore.

But they would be a week further away from home. Her parents were often distant and distracted, having decided long ago that she would learn to take care of herself more quickly if only they gave her the room to do so, but surely even they would notice her being gone for an entire week. It was difficult to say how long she had already been in the Up-and-Under—day and night seemed disinclined to follow their old familiar patterns here, and happened as it suited them, but she was sure it had been at least a day. Surely her parents had noticed when she didn't return from school! And yes, sometimes she would sleep in the yard when the weather was warm, but she normally showed up for dinner before she got her pillow and went to find herself a convenient tree. So they must have realized by now that she wasn't where they expected her to be.

Avery's parents would be even worse than hers. He wasn't the sort of boy who slept in the field because he thought the stars were pretty; he was the sort who slept in his own bed every night, with his pillow tucked just so under his head and his laundry already in the basket, tidied away and ready for the wash. There was no way that his mother and father could possibly have overlooked his absence. Adding another week to their waiting seemed cruel.

But then, it wasn't like there had been any guarantee they'd find the Queen of Wands in that week, and if she was here, somewhere on the Saltwise Sea, having a boat made it much more likely that they'd be able to locate her.

"Get us shoes, please," said Zib. "We'll wait here, we promise."

Jibson looked at her warily, waiting for some sign that she was trying to trick him. Finally, he nodded and said, "I'll be right back." He slipped out of the cabin, leaving the door to bang shut behind him.

As soon as he was gone, the Crow Girl climbed up to one of the top bunks and said, "I don't *want* to be a sailor! I don't like having wet feathers!"

"You won't," said Niamh soothingly. "As long as we're here, you won't have feathers at all."

That didn't seem to help as much as she had intended it to. The Crow Girl glanced at the door, as anxious as a fox with its leg caught in a trap, and shrank deeper into the corner of the bunk, huddling in on herself.

"Well, we're here now, and we need to make the best of it," said Avery. He sat down on one of the lower bunks, smiling a bit to find the bed well-made, the covers tucked in tightly at the corners and the whole thing smelling distantly of laundry soap. It was nice to learn that pirates knew about laundry. He had always assumed that a pirate ship, if such things still existed, would be filthy and crawling with rats. Well, this ship was perfectly clean, and he hadn't seen a single rat since they'd arrived. Perhaps this wouldn't be so terrible after all.

"Indeed we do," said Niamh, climbing up to the other top bunk. "It wouldn't do to have the sea decide to take us all for liars."

"Can the sea really reach the lake where your home is?" asked Zib earnestly.

"It can," said Niamh. "It doesn't, for the most part, because our lake is one of the coldest places in the entire world, and the sea doesn't like to be so cold as all that. Oceans aren't fond of freezing, in the main. But it can, and if my parents should hear that I'm not only still alive, but that I've become so corrupted by the land that I've started refusing to pay my debts, they would die of the shame, and no daughter wants to kill her mother with simple selfishness."

"No," agreed Zib, who was learning to take everything in the Up-and-Under literally, since no one here ever seemed to say anything they didn't think could at least be possible. She sat on the remaining lower bunk, feeling oddly reassured when she saw Avery sitting across from her. Yes, it was good to be at floor level together, if it meant they wouldn't be parted even by that much.

The door swung open again as Jibson returned, a wooden crate in his arms. "Here," he said, dropping it on the cabin floor. It rattled and clanked. "Your shoes."

"Shoes?" asked Zib, bewildered. "Shoes don't clank like that."

"These ones do," said Jibson. "There's a pair for each of you. Move quickly if you want time to eat before the captain calls you back on deck. We run a tight ship here, and everyone works." He took a step back, clearly expecting them to go for the box. When none of them moved, he crossed his arms and demanded, "Well? Are none of you hungry? Move if you want to be fed today!"

Zib slipped out of her bunk and stood, crossing the room to open the box and pull out one of the pairs of shoes. They resembled the dancing slippers she'd had when she was younger, when one of her grandmothers had believed she might be coaxed into appropriate activities for a little girl. But instead of being made of leather or canvas or any of the other materials she considered sensible for shoes, they were made of solid iron, heavy and dull in her hands.

"Iron?" she asked, bemused.

"Iron belongs to the King of Coins," said Jibson. "He owns all the metals. Gold and silver and suchlike. Iron, though . . . iron he has the least use for, for he wishes to put none of his own people in chains, and he wishes to give the other monarchs no ability to put his people in chains either. So he keeps it for himself, save when he can put it to other uses. The captain called for shoes, and he saw a chance to spend his iron in productive ways. Shoes. Put them on. Keep yourself safe from the splendors of the sea."

"If you say so," said Zib, and sat on the edge of her bunk, sliding the shoes over her feet. Then she blinked, looking surprised, and stood again. "They fit so well!" she said. "It's like they're not there at all. Avery, you have to get a pair!"

Avery, who had been wishing for shoes since losing his, grabbed a pair of shoes from the pile and stepped into them. They had no shine to them at all; they were dull gray metal that seemed, if anything, even duller after they were on his feet. He looked at them and thought they could never be polished to a proper sheen, no, they would always be flat sheets of unyielding metal.

But they fit his feet so perfectly that they scarcely seemed to weigh them down at all, and he stayed standing as he beckoned for Niamh and the Crow Girl to come down from their bunks. "I'm hungry," he said reasonably. "You need to be wearing shoes before we can all have breakfast. Come get shoes."

"I've never worn shoes," said Niamh, climbing cautiously down. "We don't need them in the city beneath the lake, and on land I've always walked barefoot."

"I don't wear shoes," said the Crow Girl, doing the same. "I have too many feet for that, and only my feather dress can go to crows and still come back again after. I would shred them into a hundred pieces, or leave them lonely in the road, if I tried wearing shoes."

"Put them on anyway," said Avery.

Both girls donned their own shoes, grimacing at the feeling of something wrapped so tight around their toes, but they didn't kick them off again, and that was good enough for Avery. He turned to Jibson.

"We're all wearing shoes now," he said. "Can we have breakfast?"

"Yes," said Jibson, and led them out of the cabin, back into the hold of the ship.

Now, there is no "right" way to construct a pirate ship. Some of them are lean and fast, intended for vicious attacks and swift robberies. They are the sailing sharks of the sea. For all that her name was fleet and fine, the *Windchaser* was not one of those ships. She was plump and overbuilt, riding low in the water from the weight of the cabins and walkways clogging her hold, taking up space that a better pirate ship might have devoted to stolen goods and cargo. For while she was a remarkable vessel that had seen her crew through many a storm and terrible hardship, she was a very poor pirate ship, and should not be used as an ideal for their design.

A long catwalk led from the cabin the children had been assigned to a line of doors that looked like something from a hotel. Delicious smells wafted from behind the door in the center. "The mess," said Jibson, somewhat needlessly, as he approached it and pulled it open, revealing a room that looked too large to have fit inside the ship. At least a dozen sailors were already there, seated at long wood tables. They ignored the open door, attention fixed on the plates and bowls in front of them.

"This way," said Jibson, and led the children further on, to a wooden table where an older woman was stirring a trough of eggs with a large spoon. A platter of bacon sat nearby, next to a tureen of oatmeal. "Maddy, I've brought you our new crew members. Can you see that they're all fed properly? The captain wants them strong enough to work off their debts to her."

"Hungry children?" asked Maddy. "You bring me hungry children, and you question whether I can feed them?"

"Yes, because I've never brought you hungry children before," said Jibson. "Can you?"

Maddy rolled her eyes, and shook her spoon at him, splattering bits of egg on the table. "Away with you now, before I give you such a walloping that you don't remember up from down. Go, go. Yes, I can feed hungry children, and you're a fool for asking me in the first place. Go."

"Thank you, Maddy," said Jibson, already moving back toward the door. Avery shot him an almost-panicked look, and Jibson smiled, flapping his hands at the group in a gesture that indicated they should move closer to the food. "Maddy will get you sorted. Come up to the deck when you're done. I have work to do. Goodbye!" And he was out the door, leaving them alone in a room full of strangers.

Not that Jibson wasn't effectively a stranger, but this seemed somehow like a betrayal, as if the person responsible for them being here no longer cared about their welfare. Maddy knocked her spoon against the tureen of eggs. All four children turned, wide-eyed and solemn, to stare at her.

"You look like hungry ones, and that's a truth I'll give you for free," she said. "Smooth those faces and find your smiles, I'm not going to do you any harm. This is my mess, and you're welcome in it as long as you don't pour rosemary in my eggs or set fire to the ship. We serve twice a day, morning and evening, and there's usually bread or cheese or the like if you need something in the middle—growing children always eat more than anyone expects them to."

Her hands were busy as she spoke, dishing up scrambled egg, bacon, and oatmeal onto four separate plates. To the first she added a sprinkle of salt; to the last she added a spoonful of what looked like brown sugar mixed with raisins. She picked up the first two plates, offering them to Avery and Zib.

"Eat, eat," she urged, voice going surprisingly gentle. "All four of you, eat. The captain will have you hard at work soon enough, and you'll regret it if you don't. Work goes more slowly when your stomach's empty."

However long they had been in the Up-and-Under, they hadn't had a hot meal in the entire time, only fish and bread and flavor fruit and bonberries. Zib's stomach gave a mighty growl, and almost before she could realize she was doing it, she had reached out and grabbed the plate that was intended for her. Avery did the same. Maddy passed the remaining two plates to Niamh and the Crow Girl.

"There's no milk, and I'm sorry for that," said Maddy, expression softening into something welcoming and kind. "But there's orange juice, in the pitchers on the tables. Be sure to drink up. Scurvy is the true scourge of the sea, and that's no lie."

"Yes, ma'am," said Avery. "Thank you, ma'am."

"Aren't you the polite one!" Maddy beamed, leaning forward to chuck his chin with one leathery finger. "Go eat, all of you."

The children moved to the nearest table and sat, well away from the chatting, feasting pirates. Niamh promptly picked up her bacon and moved it to the Crow Girl's plate, while the Crow Girl scraped her eggs onto Niamh's plate. Avery and Zib blinked at them.

"Eggs come from birds, and I'm not a cannibal," said the Crow Girl.

"There's too much salt in bacon for my stomach," said Niamh. "Too much of me is water, and not an inch of me is ocean."

"Oh," said Zib, and picked up her spoon, filling her mouth with oatmeal.

Oatmeal is a difficult thing. Done right, it can be delicious, filled with interesting textures while remaining unchallenging enough to be easy on the mouth. Done poorly, it becomes a viscous mass with no discernable qualities of its own. Suspicion in the face of a stranger's oatmeal is understandable.

Zib's eyes brightened as she swallowed, and she set herself to wolfing down her oatmeal as quickly as she could, giving every indication of pleasure and satisfaction. The Crow Girl reached cautiously for a piece of Zib's bacon. Zib whacked her hand with the spoon and kept eating, almost too fast to taste what she was gulping down.

Avery, in contrast, began with his eggs, but was soon eating as quickly and determinedly as Zib. The Crow Girl ate everything on her plate mixed together, which wasn't much, since she had only bacon and oatmeal, and Niamh ate in small, civilized bites, stretching her meal out well past the others.

When Zib ran out of oatmeal, she started on her eggs, and when she ran out of eggs, she reached for the nearest pitcher, which was heavy and cold and sloshed as she moved it, sending the sharp, sweet smell of oranges into the air. Oranges were expensive, and orange juice a rare treat at home. She didn't understand how a pirate ship could have pitchers of the stuff on every table, and as she filled the waiting cups, she didn't care to understand.

It tasted as good as it smelled, tart and sweet at the same time, delicious enough that she gulped it down greedily and filled her cup a second time. Then the second cup was gone as well, and while she would have enjoyed a third, her stomach felt as tight and distended as a drum, so full of breakfast that she could practically burst. Zib slid off the bench, her iron shoes hitting the floor with a clatter, and said, "Well? Are you ready?"

"I'm still eating," said Avery.

"Me, too," said Niamh.

"I'm ready!" The Crow Girl stood, picking up her empty plate, and asked, "Where do we go?"

"Up, Jibson said," said Zib. To Avery, she said, "I'll see you on deck." It wasn't that she was in a particular hurry to get to work; it was that to children like Zib and the Crow Girl, idleness is poison. There is always the need to be moving, to be searching, to be *doing,* whatever form that doing happens to take.

It can be frustrating, both to adults and to other children who lack that essential need for motion, to spend time with one of the doing children. Perhaps that was why Niamh and Avery merely waved, not taking their attention away from their breakfasts. Zib and the Crow Girl carried their empty plates back to Maddy, placing them in the basin that she waved them toward, and then they were off, taking all that restless energy out the door and into the hold of the ship.

Zib dashed along the catwalk to a narrow stairway that wound its way upward into the dimness of the hold. The Crow Girl followed close on her heels, nearly stumbling in her fine iron shoes, which were, after all, unfamiliar on her feet. If she had ever worn shoes, it had been before she traded her name for a hundred beating wings, and she had no memory of it.

At the top of the stairs was a narrow wooden door with a small hatch set in the top. The door refused to open when Zib tugged on it. She scowled and whacked the heel of her hand against the wood. "Stupid door," she complained. "Stupid pirates. How are we supposed to go up on deck and work if we can't get *out*?"

She didn't sound concerned. Why should she have? If she was locked in, it was with her traveling companions, and with fine new iron shoes on her feet, and with a whole mess hall full of food served by a woman who reminded her of her grandmother. Not exactly, but enough so that she couldn't imagine being afraid of her. No, there was nothing to be concerned about here. This was just another part of the adventure.

Something behind the door made a sound. It was small and weak and pleading, like it didn't expect to be heard. Zib's eyes widened. She tried to open the door again. It refused to budge.

"Try the hatch," said the Crow Girl, both wary and excited. New things were always her favorite things, for they were the things that provided the most opportunity to *do*. Crows are curious creatures, and whoever the Crow Girl had once been must have been curious, too, or she would not have been able to so easily take the murder into her heart.

Zib nodded, eyes wide, and reached up to gingerly

slide the hatch aside. It revealed a small, dark room, with patches of straw on the floor and a high window on one wall, open to let the morning sun stream in.

And there, in the middle of the straw and squalor, was a woman.

She was not young, being clearly adult. She was not old, being clearly younger than Zib's mother. She was underfed, thin enough that the sharp angles of her collarbones showed obviously through her skin. She sat at the center of what Zib was already thinking of as her cell, arms wrapped around herself and head bowed, so that her snowy hair fell to cover her face. She was wrapped in rags, tattered brown canvas rags that looked as if they might have been salvaged from a damaged sail. Zib gasped. The woman raised her head.

Zib struggled not to gasp again. The woman's eyes were huge, seeming to take up the entirety of her thin, pale face. They were the color of water in the shallows, almost clear, but with hints of blue buried in what little depth they had, as if they confused the light into refracting off them incorrectly. She looked at Zib. Zib looked at her. She wiped her eyes with the back of her hand before standing, slowly, on shaking legs, and taking a step toward the door.

"Please," she said, in a voice as low and sweet as the tide rolling in across the marshes. "Please, have you come to let me out? Please."

"I can't," said Zib. "The door won't open, and I don't have the key."

"Alas wears it at her belt, always," said the woman. "She locked me here when she decided she had no further use for me, but I haven't hurt her, you have to believe me. I haven't hurt anyone. All I wanted to do was see the world."

"I'm sorry," said Zib. "I can't steal from the captain. This is her ship, and I'm promised to serve her for the next week." It felt profoundly wrong, telling a prisoner that she couldn't help them; it felt like being the sort of person who stood by and watched while bullies picked on smaller children, and who was in many ways no better than a bully themselves, because if they'd been better than a bully, they would have helped. But she had been told, over and over again, to respect her elders, and to obey the rules when she went to someone else's home, and this was Alas's home, wasn't it? If she let this woman out, she would be both disrespecting her elders and violating the rules of someone else's home. And that would be very bad, bad and disobedient and wrong. She would be in ever so much trouble if she did something like that.

But trouble aside, it wasn't right to leave someone locked up cold and alone and scared, with nothing proper to eat or drink, in a tiny little room. Locking someone in had always seemed to Zib to be the very worst of punishments, the sort of thing that should absolutely be reserved for the very worst of crimes, like killing, since someone who'd been killed would be locked in a little pine box forever. That was why she didn't move away from the hatch.

"I'm Lýpi," said the woman, moving closer to the door. She moved slowly, not seeming to have the strength for anything else, and her eyes as she watched Zib were the eyes of someone watching a wild animal, hoping that it wouldn't run away before it could be reached. "What's your name?"

"I'm—" Zib began, and stopped as the Crow Girl grabbed her arm and yanked, pulling her away from the hatch, breaking her connection to the stranger. She turned on her friend, relieved at the familiarity of her irritation. "*What?*" she demanded, when what she meant was "thank you" and "let's run away, I'm afraid."

"You can't give her your name," said the Crow Girl, as if it were the most reasonable statement in the world. "When you give your name away, sometimes you lose it, and if you lose your name, who are you going to be?"

Zib frowned. "I told the captain and Jibson my name and you didn't object then," she said. "Why now?"

"Because then was in the daylight and the open, and then was in the dischargement of a debt, and then we weren't standing in front of a locked door in the belly of a pirate ship talking to a stranger," said the Crow Girl. "Some people are never strangers, even if you haven't met them before. Some people are always strangers, even if you live with them for a hundred years. This woman feels like the second sort of person, and if you give her your name, maybe she'll gulp it down and keep it for her own. You can't give her your name."

"All right," said Zib, shaking off the Crow Girl's grasp. "All right. I won't give her my name, all right?"

"All right," said the Crow Girl, and stepped back.

Zib moved back in front of the hatch. The woman was much closer now, and Zib flinched away when their eyes met. "H-hello," she said.

"I could hear you and your friend talking," said the woman. "You're not very good at keeping secrets if that was you trying."

"Then you know I'm not going to give you my name," said Zib. She was still more scared and shy than bold, but the nice thing about boldness is that sometimes it can pretend to be bigger than it is. Even make-believe boldness can fill a room when it has to, and Zib was pretending as hard as she could.

"I suppose that's so," said the woman—Lýpi, a name that had a lilt to it that made Zib think of summer winds and sunlight on the sea. "If you won't tell me your name, will you help me?"

"I don't know," said Zib, and her voice rang with simple honesty. She stepped back from the hatch, saying, "I don't think it's right to lock people away, but I don't have the key," before she closed it.

A low, despairing wail rose from the other side of the door. Zib shivered and hurried down the stairs, the Crow Girl at her heels. As they reached the bottom, the mess door opened and Avery and Niamh appeared. They blinked at their companions, seeming surprised to still find them belowdecks. "Did you get lost?" asked Avery.

"No," said Zib. She turned to gesture at the stairs, and stopped as she realized there were no stairs behind them, only the long sweep of the catwalk extending toward the other side of the ship. ". . . yes," she amended. "I suppose we did."

"Follow me, then," said Niamh, and started walking. The other three fell in step behind her, Avery contentedly, Zib and the Crow Girl confused. Both of them stole glances back over their shoulders as they walked, but found no sign of the mysterious stairway with the cell at the top. It was gone, as if it had never been there at all.

Niamh led them to a narrower, newer stairway, this one with bannisters polished until it seemed impossible that they could ever be the source of a snag or splinter. She started up it, and they followed, up the stairs to a door, which she pushed open to reveal the deck of the ship. Sailors moved back and forth, carrying ropes, nets, and other items from one location to the next. Niamh stepped out into the sunlight. Again, the others followed.

No sooner were they all outside than a shadow fell across them and Captain Álas appeared, hands on her hips, feet spread to mirror the width of her shoulders. Zib couldn't help seeing the bundle of keys at her waist, and looked away, feeling inexplicably unwell.

"Here you all are, properly fed and properly

shod," bellowed the captain. "Are you ready to get to work?"

"Yes, ma'am," said Avery. The rest nodded.

"Good," said the captain. She pointed to Niamh. "You know the way water works. You'll be swabbing the deck until it sparkles in the sun. I have a bucket and a mop for you." She pointed to the Crow Girl. "We need to check the knots at the top of the rigging, so you're going to climb up with Jibson and make sure everything is properly tied off." She pointed to Zib. "Maddy needs help down in the mess, getting all the dishes clean before dinner time." She pointed to Avery. "I want you in my quarters. Sailors are terrible about putting books back where they find them, and you're going to sort through my library and put it back the way it's meant to be. Do any of you have any questions?"

The Crow Girl put up her hand and said, anxiously, "I'm afraid of heights."

"But you're made of birds," said the captain. "Birds aren't afraid of heights."

"You said I'm not allowed to be birds while I'm on the ship," said the Crow Girl. "Birds may not be afraid of heights, but girls sure can be, especially when they're girls who know how easy it is for things to go splash when they fall out of the sky. Sometimes that's how we open jars and things that we can't manage with our beaks. We pick them up and carry them as high as we can, and then we just . . . let go."

"You're not made of glass," said the captain crossly. "You'll climb. Does anyone else have any questions?"

"I like to climb," said Zib. "It's easier to get me to climb than it is to keep me from climbing. Could the Crow Girl and I trade jobs, please?"

"No," snapped the captain. "She isn't made of glass, and you aren't made of sugar. You can wash a few dishes, and she can climb a few ropes. All of you, get to work! This isn't a pleasure cruise!" She went stomping off down the deck, her own iron shoes clattering against the wood.

Niamh and Avery exchanged a glance, shrugged, and went off to begin working on their perfectly suitable, perfectly acceptable tasks. Zib and the Crow Girl's shared look lasted longer, and when they turned to walk away from each other, it was with slumped shoulders and dragging feet. Captain Alas couldn't have chosen jobs they would like less if she'd been trying, because even if she'd been trying, she didn't know them well enough to understand just how upsetting the jobs she'd assigned them would be.

For the Crow Girl, the fear of falling without wings to catch herself was all-consuming and inescapable. It would make her fingers clumsy and slow her completion of a task she had never asked for in the first place. Being so close to the sky and unallowed to fly away would be torture for her, every moment, and entirely unfair.

For Zib, being on something as exciting as a pirate ship, chasing the horizon and racing the waves, but forced into a windowless room to wash dishes with a woman who already reminded her of her grandmother, was the next thing to torture. "Torture" is a big word to involve in a conversation about doing dishes; most people, when they hear it, will think of knives and needles and fiery brands pressed against unprotected skin. But the truth is, torture will take different forms for different people. Sometimes it can be hunger, or thirst, or cruel words. In Zib's case, it was the denial of adventure and the forced adherence to a part she had been refusing to play since the first time someone had spoken the word "girl" in her hearing.

It seemed ridiculous to her that anyone could look at her and think she was the sort of child who was suited to laundry and sweeping and eventual motherhood, and all because of a name she had never chosen for herself. "Girl" was a name for another kind of creature, something she was not and would have no idea how to go about becoming, even if she wanted to. If they needed a child to cook and clean and organize, they should speak to Avery, who seemed to find comfort in such actions, and was still lamenting the lost shine in his shoes.

When Zib arrived in the mess hall, she found it empty of sailors; only Maddy was there, up to her elbows in a trough of soapy water. "It's a long time before dinner, missy," she said, and laughed to herself, as if she had said something genuinely hilarious. "What can I do for you?"

"The captain told me to come down here and help

you clean up," said Zib. Whether she was making no effort to hide her misery, or simply had so much misery that it was overflowing her fragile barriers and cascading absolutely everywhere, was impossible to say.

Maddy looked at her gravely. "Ah," she said finally. "I see. There's always one, whenever we get new recruits."

"One what?" asked Zib.

"One who wants the sea so badly that the captain feels the need to remind them it doesn't belong to them—not yet. Maybe it could, if they work hard and stay on past their initial term, but it doesn't just because they stepped onto the deck. So you want the sea, eh, little girl? Does the sea want you?"

"I don't know." Zib clomped across the room to where Maddy was working, rolling up her sleeves before plunging her hands into the hot, soapy water. Hating the chore had never been enough to keep her away from it, and she knew what to do. "I don't know if anywhere wants me."

"The Up-and-Under clearly wants you, even if America doesn't," said Maddy, in a sage tone. Zib whipped around to stare at her, and Maddy smiled. "What, you think you're the only American child to find their way to the Forest of Borders? I thought I knew your accent. We don't only get American children, of course. I know America likes to believe itself to be the best at everything, but we have no monopoly on unexpected borders. I know a very nice fisherman who came originally from Canada. He'll trade you a nursery rhyme for a cod if you can think of one that he's forgotten, or never knew in the first place. And there's a woman who was born in Mexico City who makes and sells lace in the Impossible City. Oh, don't stare so! Time is happening here, the same way it's happening everywhere else, and while you can hide from a great many things, you can't hide from growing up just by going to another country. That would be patently ridiculous, and wouldn't make any sense at all. How are the crops to ripen and the fields to be brought in if nothing's getting any older? Everyone would starve to death waiting for the wheat."

"But what about your parents?" croaked Zib. "What about going home where you belong?"

"That's a loaded question, isn't it?" asked Maddy. "If I belonged where I'd begun, why would the wall have come for me to climb? I don't think it goes looking for children who belong where they are. I think it goes looking for children who have something to learn about the way the world works, and who can find that lesson in the Up-and-Under."

"How can a wall go looking for *anything*?"

"Spoken as if you haven't been chasing the improbable road! Don't try to deny it, even if you would; there's a look to road-walkers, and you have it, all four of you, although there's less in your crow. She doesn't know quite who she is or wants to be any longer, and it's going to take some great trial for her to remember, make no mistake. Walls can do as walls can do, and you can do these dishes until the captain sees fit to let you free, and I can dry my hands for a moment, since I have a helper." Maddy's smile was sympathetic. "I know you hate it, poppet, but it won't be forever, and the sea will be there when you're done. The sea is always there. She changes her face, she's not always kind, but she's always there."

"I saw a woman," Zib began, hesitantly.

Maddy's face hardened. "That stairway *isn't* always there, and if you see it again, you steer clear. Do you understand me? There's nothing good to be accomplished by climbing where you're not welcome. Listen, and mind me well."

"Yes, ma'am," said Zib, and kept washing dishes, while through the wall of the pirate ship came the softly whispered singing of the sea.

SEVEN

ON STORMY SEAS

There were as many dishes to be washed as there were sailors on the ship, which is to say, more dishes than Zib had ever seen outside of the holidays, when it seemed as if every distant cousin she could name had made it their personal goal in life to drown her in chipped plates and bowls with smears of gravy still clinging to the rim. The washing of one dish is much like the washing of another, and so we leave Zib to her unwanted, unenvied task, washrag in one hand and flatware in the other. She'll be fine.

Instead, we rise up through the body of the ship to the deck, where Niamh patiently swabs, the mop in her hand well taller than she is, saying nothing to the pirates who tromp by, their bootsoles staining the freshly swabbed wood, forcing her to do it over and over and over again. If this frustrates her, she gives no sign. She only continues in her work. There is a smile on her face, and she has the sea air combing through her hair like the patient fingers of a loving mother; like Zib, she'll be fine.

Higher still, the rigging, and we find the Crow Girl, still in her borrowed iron shoes, clinging to the rope in terrified determination. She has only checked three of the knots she was sent to the heights to check. Every time she reaches for the fourth, the same wind that strokes Niamh's hair blows through the rigging and sets it to shaking, and she cries out and clings harder, clearly terrified of falling. Jibson is there with her, trying to coax her into working faster, growing increasingly frustrated with his inability to get through her fear. She'll be up there for hours if the captain insists the job be finished before her descent.

In the small building behind the wheel, however, there is a room we have not yet seen: the captain's quarters, which are easily three times the size of the room our four children have been assigned to share, and opulent in a way that even a rich man's room on land might envy, with walls papered in rich brocade and the floor softened by piles upon piles of rugs. The bed is draped in heavy velvet curtains, and as Avery stepped into the room, he resolutely does not look at it. If he looked at the bed, he might remember his exhaustion, and if he remembered his exhaustion, he wouldn't finish the work he'd been assigned to do.

One entire wall of the cabin was dedicated to tall

oak bookshelves, crammed with more books than he had ever seen outside of a library. True to the captain's word, more than half of them were out of order, and it seemed like every time he put a book back where it belonged, he found two more that needed to be moved. There was a clever ladder attached to the book wall, with wheels that moved soundlessly when he pushed against it, and he didn't have to worry about anything being out of reach.

He was less sure why a pirate ship needed to have so many books, but they were here, and that meant they needed to be treated with respect. Treating books with respect was something that came easy to him, having been drilled into him by every adult he'd ever known. One by one, he stroked the covers, straightened the spines, and moved the books into their places, making order out of chaos, and found that the world was a better place for being so corrected.

He was reaching for a weighty tome bound in purple damask when the ship gave a mighty lurch and he was nearly knocked from his ladder. Confused, Avery climbed down to the floor and moved toward the cabin door, intending to find out what was going on. The ship lurched again, this time knocking him to the floor, where the rugs padded his fall.

On the rigging outside, the Crow Girl's greatest fear was finally realized, as the second lurch knocked her out of the rigging and she plummeted toward the deck below. She clawed frantically at the air as she fell, and Avery or Zib would have recognized the position of her arms as the one she regularly assumed right before bursting into birds. But her body remained a single contiguous piece, and before she was halfway down, she had stopped flailing and allowed herself to simply fall, plummeting peacefully toward the deck below.

Niamh dropped her mop and grabbed her bucket, dashing its contents into the air below the Crow Girl. The water froze there, still liquid, but somehow floating, and came together into a vast bubble that seemed far too large to have been contained in Niamh's bucket. The Crow Girl struck the surface with a splash, and was pulled inside, her eyes snapping open as she realized that she had hit water and not unforgiving wood. She sat upright with a gasp, her head breaking the surface of the water. Niamh snapped her fingers. The bubble gently set the Crow Girl down on the deck before retreating back into the bucket, where it curled, unmoving.

Once again perfectly dry, the Crow Girl stared at Niamh, eyes very wide indeed. "I didn't know you could *do* that!" she squawked.

"I didn't need to before," said Niamh, with a shrug. "And I can't, always. The water has to know me before it will listen to me. I've been working with this water for hours now." The water in the bucket gave a little glorping bubble, as if to agree with her.

"All hands to stations," barked the captain, striding by. "We have a devil of a storm rolling in, and there's no room for idleness in a squall!"

"We don't have stations," said Niamh. The sky had started to darken as the captain spoke, and was already the color of a deep blue-black bruise, the kind that stretched all the way down to the bone. The clouds hung heavy and low against the horizon, closing in with impossible quickness.

Captain Alas looked at the children as if she had never seen them before, a confusion that failed to lift when her cabin door banged open and Avery came running out. He looked up at the sky with wide eyes, and asked, "Is there a storm coming?"

The captain nodded, seeming to snap partially out of her fugue, and said, "Aye, a bad one. As you children have no stations yet, get below. When the wind blows, it'll take anything that's not nailed down, and you're all small enough to serve as souvenirs." She strode away, already shouting again, ordering sailors hither and yon.

The Crow Girl grabbed Avery and Niamh by the hands, pulling them toward the door that would take them into the belly of the ship. "Hurry, hurry, hurry," she chattered. "I don't want to be blown away, not when I can't . . ." She stopped, a brief look of horror flickering across her face, and bit her lip.

Avery, who hadn't seen her fall, asked, "Can't what?"

Niamh simply nodded, and said, "She can't be birds right now."

"How is that possible? She *is* birds."

"Surely the captain would understand if she was birds to save herself."

"I don't mean she doesn't want to disobey. She *can't*," said Niamh.

"'Alas said her magic would keep the Crow Girl in one piece, but not that it would *hurt* her. Surely she can be crows if not being crows would *hurt* her."

Niamh grabbed Avery's hand and pulled him along with her as she ran for the door. The Crow Girl followed, moving just as quickly as she could in her tight-fitting iron shoes. Niamh flung the door open to find Zib standing on the other side, still holding a ladle dripping with soapy water. Zib's eyes widened at the sight of her friends. Niamh shoved past her, letting go of Avery's hand once they were safely below. The Crow Girl slammed the door.

"Storm coming in," explained Niamh. "Pretty bad. The captain wanted us all to get to safety before it hit."

Zib squealed excitement and dove for the door. The Crow Girl stopped her with an arm like an iron bar, knocking her back a foot. Zib pouted at her, denied the excitement she so craved.

"I've been outside in storms before," she wheedled.

"But not on a pirate ship in the middle of the Saltwise Sea," said Niamh.

It was the wrong reply. Zib nodded, enthusiasm clearly growing. "I want to see how it's different!" she said. "I want to see how tall the waves can get, and whether the lightning will go for the mast! Let me out, let me see!"

"No," said Avery, face pale as whey and hands

shaking slightly. The things that excited Zib so much terrified him; what if the lightning *did* strike the mast, what would happen to the sailors who were in the rigging and struggling to control the sail? What if the waves got so tall that they swamped the side of the ship and washed everything away? What if the four of them went back up when the storm was over and they were the only ones left in the whole world? It was all too much and too big to think about, and so he folded it inward on itself, twisting confusion and ignorance into something that felt very much like a knife. "You don't want to see it. You're not brave enough. Even the sailors are scared. How could one little girl not be even more afraid? You have to stay down here with us. With the rest of the *children*."

Zib took a step backward, staring at Avery in dismay. She didn't want him to think of her like that. She didn't want him to say such things. She wanted him to be her friend, who had saved her from the King of Cups, and to be on her side. Few enough people had ever been on her side. She'd been so sure that Avery was one of them.

"That's mean," she said, in a small voice. "You take that back."

"Why?" he asked. "It's true. The captain sent us all down here to hide with you, because this storm is too big and too scary for little kids like us. That means me *and* you."

"We're not little kids!" she protested. "We faced

down the Bumble Bear and we found the skeleton key and we—"

"And we paid for those things," he said. "Nothing's free on this side of the wall! Maybe nothing was free back home either, but there, we had our parents to stand between us and whatever it all cost. We can't go out in that storm, Zib! We'll be blown away, or *you'll* be blown away, because I'm not going to risk it, and then I'll have to walk the improbable road without you!" He didn't say "alone," although that was the word he wanted; walking the improbable road with Niamh and the Crow Girl, who belonged to the Up-and-Under and would never wish themselves away to anyplace else, felt like walking it alone. He didn't want that. He wanted Zib. He just didn't know how to say that without pushing her further away.

Zib looked at him, lip quivering and hair seeming to deflate in her sorrow. Avery looked stubbornly back, his body still set between her and the only door. Finally, she spun on her heel and ran down the catwalk, vanishing into the dimness in the hold. Avery let out a long breath, seeming to deflate in on himself, as the Crow Girl punched him in the shoulder. He turned to blink at her.

"What?" he asked.

"I'm not very good at being a person," she said. "I think I lost the knack of it somewhere along the line, if I ever had the knack. But even I know you were just very cruel to her, and you shouldn't be cruel to your friends when you have any other choice in the world. You need to go and apologize."

"What?" asked Avery again, disbelieving this time, like he couldn't understand what she was talking about. "Why should I apologize for telling her that she can't go outside in a storm and get herself killed? That's just common sense! Would you be asking me to apologize if I'd let her go out and be swept away?"

"No, because we wouldn't let you do that," said Niamh. "There's a difference between speaking truly and being cruel. You were cruel. You chose words you knew would hurt her, and you slung them like stones. Words have power. If they didn't, we wouldn't carry them the way we do. Sometimes a word is the only weapon you have. Go apologize."

Avery looked at Niamh and the Crow Girl, unified against him, and swallowed the urge to stomp one iron-clad shoe against the catwalk in frustration. Couldn't they see that he was lost and tired and confused, just like Zib was? He was on a pirate ship in the middle of the ocean, and he'd finally been starting to feel like he might be able to fit in here when the stupid storm had come along and knocked everything off-kilter again. His thoughts were like the books in the captain's cabin, all out of order and scattered across the floor.

But Niamh and the Crow Girl were still scowling at him, and so he turned and began to make his grudging way down the walk. His shoes clattered with every step he took, and it was difficult not to resent them as well, for being so loud and awkward that there was no possible way to approach quietly. Zib would have plenty of time to run farther away from him, if she decided that she wanted to. He could be hunting for her forever.

As he walked, he started to feel a little bad about what he'd said. He'd been telling the truth, sure, but he'd also been choosing the parts of the truth he focused on to be as pointed as possible. He'd been being mean, and he'd known it even as he was doing it, and he hadn't been able to quite tell himself to stop. It was like the mean Avery and the Avery who knew Zib was already his best and truest friend, and probably would be for the rest of both their lives, were different people, split almost entirely in two. He didn't know where that other Avery had come from, but he wanted to hope that he wouldn't come back again the next time he was afraid.

Everyone has another self inside them who comes out when they feel the time is right. For most people, that second self is summoned by fear or panic, which are similar and not the same. For others, that second self is brought out by the feeling of love or safety. The trick with second selves is not learning how to get rid of them—which can't be done, no matter how hard a person tries—but finding a way to teach them to be kinder, one simple step at a time. Even second selves can be taught the way of walking through the world transmuting harm into healing; even second selves can grow.

Avery looked at his second self and was ashamed. So when the walkway he had been following Zib along became a flight of stairs, he was well-prepared to climb them, and at the top he found a narrow wooden door with a hatch set into it at just his eye-height. That struck him as somewhat odd; he was, after all, shorter than the average pirate by a good bit, and what use was a peephole too short for most people to use it?

There was no sign of Zib. He could hear the wind howling from the other side of the door; the storm had closed the distance between itself and the ship, and the squall was now well and truly underway. But there was another sound, beneath the storm, a more familiar, more painful sound: when he pressed his ear against the wood, Avery could hear a woman weeping. She sounded pained, like she had been crying for days with no hope of stopping, and had no hope of stopping even now. For her tears to carry over the storm, it seemed obvious they must be powerful ones, and painful ones, and ones that should be soothed away.

"Zib?" he asked, trying the door. It refused to budge, having been locked tight. He opened the hatch, peering through into the room on the other side. "Zib, are you in there? I'm sorry about the things I said before. I didn't mean to—"

He stopped as the woman in the room raised her head and looked at him. She wasn't Zib. She was too old to be Zib, older even than the Crow Girl, as old as the girl his parents sometimes called to babysit him when they wanted to go out on the weekend. Her hair was white, like clouds in the morning, and her eyes were both huge and the color of shallow water, which was to say, they were no color at all. He had never seen a person with eyes like that, not ever once in his life.

Tears were running down her cheeks, as heavy and unceasing as the rain outside her chamber's single window.

"I-I'm sorry," he said. "I'm looking for my friend. She's my age, with hair that looks like it wants to steal anything that's not nailed down." He remained reasonably sure that Zib could produce anything she needed just by reaching into her hair and tugging it free.

The woman in the room started to shake her head before catching herself and nodding hesitantly. "I saw her before, with the black-haired girl. They came to my door. I asked them to help me. They said they couldn't. Then they closed the hatch and they went away, and they left me here. Please." She spread her hands, reaching for Avery without moving from her place on the floor. "Please don't leave me here. My name is Lýpi. I'm a person. I don't deserve to be locked up like this. I didn't do anything wrong."

"I don't think you'd deserve to be locked up even

if you had done something wrong," said Avery uncertainly. His parents didn't talk much about political things, but he had heard his father talking about the immorality of keeping people imprisoned without a proper trial. There wasn't anyplace on the pirate ship to *hold* a proper trial, and even if there had been, he couldn't see how locking someone in a tiny room all by themselves could ever be the right thing to do. If she'd committed a crime, she should have been sent to a real prison, not kept sealed away here. "But this door is locked. I don't know how I'd get you out. Even if I said I'd help you, I don't know if I could."

"The captain of this ship has the key. She wears it at her belt. If you were to get it from her, you could let me out."

Avery frowned and drew back, feeling suddenly wary. Captain Álas had been reasonable so far, giving them shoes and food and a safe place to sleep, and jobs that were not too difficult for them to do. He understood why they needed to serve her for a week, to repay her for trespassing and touching her things without asking. If he'd had the power to make anyone who snuck into his room and used his things without asking serve him for a week, he would have done it in a heartbeat. Even intangible things must be balanced if the world is to remain anything resembling fair.

"Why did she put you here?" he asked. "What did you do?"

"She wanted to forget me," said Lýpi. "She said I

wasn't a person at all, just a story of the sea, but look at me! Look at my fingers, look at my hands. These are things stories do not have, for stories do not need them! But here I am, and here I'll stay, until some clever child acquires the key and comes to let me go."

"Oh," said Avery. He paused for a moment, pondering her words, and followed it up with a mild "No," and closed the hatch again, taking a step backward. He felt like the air grew lighter as he moved, and when he was well clear of the door, he turned and fled back down the steps, intending to go as far as he needed in order to find Zib.

He nearly collided with her at the bottom of the stairway. Grabbing her upper arms to steady himself, he gasped, "Zib! I'm sorry I was mean, I was frightened of the storm and afraid that if you went outside you would be swept away and I'd never be able to find you again and you'd go to the bottom of the sea and be a drowned girl like Niamh and then you'd go live in her city at the bottom of the lake forever and leave me all alone!" His words came out in a gasping flow with no breaks for breath, so that by the end, he was wheezing, holding her to remain upright.

Zib blinked. Once, twice, and three times, before she asked, in a strangely solemn voice, "Did you see Lýpi?" Her pronunciation of the woman's name was not perfect, could have used more time to find perfection, but as she had only heard it once and did not know where the woman's accent had come from, it was as close as could reasonably have been expected.

There is nothing wrong with pronouncing a word incorrectly when you have only heard it once before, but when that word is something as personal as someone's name, it matters more that you *try*, that you listen hard for the place where each syllable bends and blurs into the next, and that if necessary, you ask for the proper pronunciation. Zib, who had been blessed from birth with a name that many people found unusual and complicated, would normally have made more of an effort, but she hadn't been able to find the stair until Avery was descending it, and besides, she was afraid to talk to her again.

"Yes," said Avery. He hesitated before adding, "She tried to convince me that she was a person, and not just a story of the sea. She said that was what the captain called her, and that I should steal the key to the room where she's been locked. But I don't know if that's the right thing to do."

"I don't know either," said Zib, sounding relieved. "She asked me to do the same thing. I suppose she must ask everyone who comes close enough to talk to her, and everyone must tell her 'no,' or she wouldn't be locked up there anymore."

"If we were supposed to stay away from her, I think the captain would have told us so," said Avery. "We could ask."

Asking adults sometimes had the opposite effect

of the one that he was looking for, but it was still the best way to learn more. Even a snapped "Don't ask about that, it's none of your concern" was better than nothing.

Zib bit her lip. "But what if she doesn't like us asking?"

"She can't put us off the ship without breaking her own bargain," said Avery. "And she can't keep us here longer just for asking a question. That wouldn't be fair. The captain cares a lot about being fair."

"Not so I've noticed," grumbled Zib, glancing at the ladle still clutched firmly in one hand.

"What?" asked Avery.

"Nothing," said Zib. "Where are the others?"

"I left them back by the entrance," said Avery. "They were really upset about me being mean to you. They sent me to apologize."

Something in Zib's face fell. "Oh," she said. "You didn't apologize because you thought you needed to?"

Avery felt suddenly small and ashamed. "No," he admitted. "But I think I had to. I feel like I had a second self who came out for a minute to be mean to you, and then as soon as he went away, I started having second thoughts that should probably have been first thoughts. I should have thought them before I said anything at all."

"I wish you'd apologized because you saw why you needed to," said Zib, with exquisite care. "But you apologized, and sometimes that has to be good enough. Let's go find them."

She walked down the path toward the door. Avery followed, head spinning. Zib had accepted his apology. Did that mean everything was good again? Were they done fighting? Had they ever been fighting in the first place? Sometimes people said mean things, but saying a mean thing didn't always mean having a fight. Fights took both people deciding they were happening to really work, otherwise it was just one person being mean for no reason.

He was still trying to decide whether it had really been a fight when they reached the end of the walkway. Niamh and the Crow Girl were still standing right where he had left them. Niamh watched the pair approach with a perfectly neutral expression on her face, as if doing anything else would be picking sides and she wasn't entirely prepared to do that yet. The Crow Girl was nowhere near as calm.

As soon as Zib reached the others, the Crow Girl flung her arms up over her head, exclaimed, "There you are! I missed you!" and embraced the smaller girl, squeezing her hard enough to knock the air out of her lungs. Zib laughed and wheezed and patted the Crow Girl on the shoulder as she tried to pull away.

"I need to *breathe,*" she protested, laughing. The Crow Girl finally let go. Zib took a step backward, out of reach, her shoulder bumping against Avery's chest. She glanced over her shoulder, looking startled, as if she had forgotten he was there.

She did forget, whispered the voice of his second self. It was low and sweet and oddly compelling, like it understood the situation better than he possibly could. *You don't matter to her. Look how quick she is to run away when she thinks there's an adventure to be had. You only climbed that wall because she talked you into it. You'd be safe home in bed right now if it weren't for her.*

The things it said were just true enough to make him want to keep listening, to make him want to believe. But that didn't mean listening or believing would have been the right choice. With a wrench that would have been difficult for many people twice his age, Avery shoved the voice of his second self as far to the back of his mind as it would go and mustered a smile for Zib, putting a hand on her arm to steady her. After a beat, Zib smiled back.

The storm was still raging outside, loudly enough that it echoed through the hull. The four of them exchanged a look.

"Let's go to our cabin," said Zib. "We have beds there. If the storm doesn't stop, we can go to sleep, and when we wake up, the storm will probably be over."

Avery, who was still exhausted from their adventures so far, nodded more vigorously than he normally would have at the prospect of going to bed in the middle of the day. Naps were for babies . . . and adventurers, he supposed. All that extra work had to mean getting some extra sleep. That was only reasonable. "I know the way from here," he said. "Come on."

Together, in a ragged, exhausted line, they walked

back to the cabin they'd been assigned and collapsed into their respective bunks. None of them intended to fall asleep, but between one heartbeat and the next, all four of them did, and no one came to wake them.

EIGHT

STORIES OF THE SEA

The ship was sailing smoothly on calm seas when the children woke again, first Niamh, then Avery and Zib almost at the same time, and finally the Crow Girl, pulling herself bodily out of a dream of soaring over endless forests filled with trees whose branches reached, in yearning welcome, toward the summer sky. They sat up, one by one, rubbing at their eyes and listening for signs that the storm was coming back. When she heard no whistle of wind or crack of thunder, Zib slid out of her bunk and grabbed her iron shoes from the floor, jamming them onto her feet.

"Storm's over!" she chirped brightly. "I bet there's food in the mess!" She didn't wait for the rest of them before she went barreling out of the cabin and down the walkway, fully rested and hence once more filled with the seemingly inexhaustible energy that had been her primary weapon against the world since she'd been born.

Moving more slowly, Avery got his own shoes on, beckoning for Niamh and the Crow Girl to follow. "We should hurry before she finds some new kind of trouble to get into," he said. His teeth felt fuzzy. He had never in his life gone this long without brushing them, and he was starting to slowly realize that his parents hadn't just been being mean when they made him pick up the toothpaste every morning and night. Soon he would be able to pet his molars like kittens, he was sure, and while he had always liked kittens, he was less sure he liked them inside his mouth.

"Whazzit?" asked the Crow Girl, sounding like she was still more than half asleep and not quite capable of making decisions for herself yet. She climbed down from her bunk, and Niamh did the same, both of them collecting their shoes and falling in behind Avery. Niamh looked the same as she always did, damp and a bit disheveled, as if she had been swept in from someplace upstream. The Crow Girl's dress was in profound disarray, feathers sticking out in all directions, and her hair was even wilder, until she could have given Zib a run for her money.

"We're going to go get food," said Avery reassuringly. Like Zib before him, he didn't name the meal, didn't say "lunch" or "dinner," because there was no way of knowing, in their windowless cabin, what meal they would be walking into.

The Crow Girl brightened, a little light coming into her eyes. "Food?" she asked hopefully.

"Food," Avery assured her, and led the pair out of the cabin, down the walkway to the mess door. There was no sign of any stairway, which seemed like a good sign; they wouldn't have to deal with an imprisoned woman who might or might not exist if the stairway to her cell wasn't there.

Avery pushed open the door to the mess, and the smell of frying cheese rushed out, savory and greasy and impossibly good. He licked his lips as he stepped inside.

As yesterday, there were sailors seated at the long tables, and Maddy was manning her station, filling plates for anyone who approached. Zib stood off to one side, chatting animatedly with the cook, a plate in her own hands. She turned when she heard the sound of iron shoes against the floor, and smiled so brightly it was like her friends were the best things she had ever seen in her life.

"It's dinner!" she said brightly, as if this were the answer to some great mystery—and in a way, perhaps it was. Either they had only been asleep for a few hours, or they had all slept an entire day away, but regardless, now they knew what time it was, or at least the vague neighborhood of what time it was, and other things could be accordingly decided. "Maddy made grilled cheese sandwiches!"

"And salad, don't forget," said Maddy. "Young things like you need to eat some greens if you want to grow big and strong. There's orange juice on the tables. Drink up. You need your vitamins when you set off to sea."

"Grilled cheese sandwiches and salad and there's bonberry pie for afters," said Zib, voice still bright enough to sound almost giddy. "Get your plates, I'll get us seats." She started for the nearest table, plate in hand.

"She's a happy one, isn't she?" asked Maddy, beginning to dish up plates for the other three. "I thought sure she'd run out and be swept off in the storm."

"So did we," admitted Avery. "I don't think Zib has ever seen an adventure she didn't want to have as quickly and completely as she possibly could."

"Well, you're good friends for stopping her. The storms we get here on the Saltwise Sea are a collision of Cups and Coins, and they cut deeper than the storms you get on the land, I think because the King of Cups doesn't like that he does not have sole claim here." Maddy shook her head, handing over the last plate. "No element is ever purely pure. There's salt in the sea, and salt comes from Coins, and there's fire in the clouds, however much the Swords will try to sweep it aside. Don't ever hold out for purity, my ducklings, unless you want to live your lives in profound disappointment."

"Yes, ma'am," said Avery, voice blank with confusion. He turned toward the table where Zib was already seated, giving Niamh a hopeful, questioning look. The drowned girl seemed to understand the Up-and-Under better than any of the rest of them, and unlike the adults, she didn't make assumptions that left holes in her explanations. Niamh caught his look and sighed, nodding, but didn't begin to speak until they were seated alongside Zib.

"The Up-and-Under is a kingdom made up of four countries," she said. "Each of them has its own ruler, and stands for its own element. So the Queen of Wands, before she disappeared, stood for the element of fire, which is how she could also be the summer incarnate, and ruled over the country of Aster. Most people call it the country of Wands, but that's not really its name."

"Why would you call a country by something that isn't its name?" asked Avery.

"Where are you from again?" asked Niamh.

"America," said Avery, and "The United States," said Zib, and Niamh nodded, looking satisfied.

"Sometimes a thing's name is too big to use all the time, because if you did, you might attract its attention," she said, like it was the most reasonable thing in the world. She picked up her fork and stabbed it into the strange, glossy lettuce of her little salad, spearing a tomato the color of the sunset. "All the countries have proper names. The Saltwise Sea is part of the country of Hyacinth—most of the country of Hyacinth, in fact, because Hyacinth is water, and this is the biggest water in all of the Up-and-Under. The

King of Coins rules over the country of Meadowsweet, and the Queen of Swords rules the country of Crocus. She hates that name so much! She says it's too small to describe her glory, and she'd change it if she could. But she won't be Queen forever, because no one is a King or Queen forever, and that means she can't change the parts of her country that came before her and will last so much longer than her. Her name and her element are both fixed. So is her season. She's winter, or she would be if she allowed herself to be, or if she ever took the Impossible City, and she'd freeze as only the cold north wind can freeze. She'd set the world in ice if she had the opportunity. She doesn't, yet, and so she can't."

Zib frowned. "But the King of Cups was where all the cold was. The Queen of Swords was just sad and lonely."

"The Queen of Swords makes monsters," said Niamh. "Never forget that. The Queen of Swords transforms things that don't suit her exactly as they are, and she's not sorry to have done it. She's never been sorry for anything in her life, not even the things that leave her sitting alone in the forest, wondering why no one loves her. She'd freeze you to the core if she had the chance, and she'd laugh when people asked her why she'd done it. Cold is more than just a little ice and snow. Spring can be so cold it burns. But in the end, spring will thaw. In the end, the King of Cups can be convinced to let his victims go."

"What about the Page of Frozen Waters?" asked Zib, and shivered. "*She* doesn't want to let her victims go."

"But she isn't the spring, or the keeper of the Cups," said Niamh. "She only has a few weapons to her name, and she doesn't claim the country. She never could. Her nature is better suited to Crocus than to Hyacinth, but she hates the Queen of Swords and refuses to serve her in any capacity, however temporary."

Zib blinked, looking faintly dazed. "I never thought there'd be so many rules to keeping a fairy tale world going."

"Child, who told you we were a fairy tale?" Niamh frowned. "Fairy tales are all about magic and morals. You won't find any morals here. Not that a parent would whisper to you at bedtime before they kiss your forehead and turn the lights out."

"But we climbed a wall that wasn't supposed to be there and fell into a country where a person can be a season and flocks of crows can turn into girls," protested Zib. "This has to be a fairy tale!"

"It doesn't *have* to be anything except for what it is," said Niamh. She took a delicate bite of her grilled cheese sandwich. "Nothing has to change its nature to suit what someone else decides it's going to be."

"Nothing?" asked the Crow Girl, in a small, surprised voice.

Niamh blinked at her, and then nodded, slowly. "Nothing," she said.

The four ate in silence after that, and all of them

cleared their plates to Maddy's satisfaction and were hence rewarded with fat, hot slices of bonberry pie. There was no cream to go with the pie, but it was fresh and buttery enough not to need anything extra.

Zib was the first to finish eating and Avery was the last, and all four of them paused to catch their breath and sip their orange juice. The whole meal had had the feeling of a pause between calamities, an opportunity to take a moment and remember that the world was not a constant case of tumbling from one crisis into the next. Now the pause was over, and it was time to go back to falling, at least for a little while. So they rose reluctantly, and delivered their plates and cutlery to be washed, Zib dancing away from the washwater like a splashed cat, while Maddy chuckled at the girl's reluctance to be roped back into the chore.

"You be good, children, and if you see any runaway dishes while you're out and about on the ship, be sure to bring them here so I can wash them up," she said.

Avery and Zib nodded, although neither of them could have said whether she was talking about dirty dishes that had been misplaced by careless sailors, or actual dishes that had somehow found the ability to run off on their own, and the four children left the mess together.

On the walkway, there was still no sign of the stairway to Lýpi's cell, and so they were able to put the question of her confinement to the side for a little while longer as they walked toward the door that would take them out onto the deck. Avery glanced at Zib, and startled. "Where's your sword?" he asked.

"What?"

"The sword Niamh pulled out of the river when you were locked in the cage. She gave it to me and you took it, because I'm not suited to swords." It was a small and simple truth that neither of them questioned. They had both learned the pointlessness of arguing with the truth. "Where is it?"

"I left it in my bunk," said Zib. "It seemed rude to walk around all day with a sword at my hip if we're among friends, and if we're not among friends, I'd rather they not look at me and think, 'that little girl has a sword, I'd best take her out first if I'm going to fight them.' I can go get it, if you think I need it."

"Oh." Avery glanced at Niamh. She was looking at the grain of the walls, apparently unconcerned. He had learned to pay attention to her reactions.

If she wasn't concerned, neither was he. He turned his attention back to Zib. "That's fine. I just realized you weren't wearing it, and that seemed strange. You like having a sword."

"I do," Zib agreed, and opened the door.

The deck was a disaster. Ropes and shreds of sail dangled everywhere, and sailors rushed back and forth as they cleaned up the damage done by the storm. The mast still stood straight and tall, which was probably the only good thing Avery could say about the scene; once the sail was mended, they would be able to keep sailing. He wasn't sure when that had become the most important thing, but it was. This was still their first day onboard, after all. They had to sail for six more before they could get back to the search for the Queen of Wands, who would be able to send them home again.

Captain Álas saw them standing in the open door and came striding in their direction. "My little cabin rats," she boomed. "I thought for sure that you'd been swept out to sea and were dining in the palace of the fishes tonight!"

"Do the fish actually have a palace?" asked the Crow Girl. "If they do, I would very much like to dine there tonight. I'm sure they can do amazing things with kelp and oysters, and oysters probably wouldn't have any place in the government of fish. They're all belly and no brain. On second thought, that might make them perfect politicians." She laughed, and if there was an element of harsh cawing in the sound, no one was going to be rude enough to point it out to her.

"I wouldn't put it past them, the slippery things," said the captain. "That's why when you miss one fish, your catch drops until you sail to different waters. They go back to their palaces and send out the word that someone's trying to catch them for the dinner table."

"Supper didn't have any fish in it," said Avery,

with the air of someone who was starting to unsnarl a great mystery. "Grilled cheese is nice, but it's strange for a ship in the middle of the sea. Is it because the fishing's been bad?"

"The fishing's been bad since I became captain of this vessel," she said. "They seem to know we're coming. We take on produce at every port, just to make up for the lack. Half of what we pillage from the King's ships goes straight into filling the bellies of my crew."

Avery privately thought that the food on offer was rich and overly fancy for a pirate ship. But as he was going to be eating it for the next six days, he wasn't going to be the one to suggest simpler fare.

Zib took a half-step forward. "Pardon me, captain, but we had something we wanted to ask you."

Captain Álas shifted her focus to Zib, previously mild expression taking on a hard edge of annoyance. Zib blinked.

"Why don't you like me?" she blurted, thoughts of the woman at the top of the stairs going quite out of her head.

She was used to people not liking her once they'd gotten to know her. She was loud and impulsive and unpredictable and *messy*. She had often thought she would have been better liked if she'd been born a boy, but when she looked down to the bottom of herself, all she ever saw was "girl." So when she wished on stars, she wished only to be better at being the thing she seemed condemned to be, and not to be something else altogether, which she sometimes thought would have been easier, if only it had been something she could believe it was possible to aspire to. So someone not liking her was far from a shock. What *was* a bit of a shock was that the captain had seemed to dislike her from the moment they met, and she was a charming little girl, with big eyes, thick lashes, and hair that seemed less "wild" and more "artful" on first meeting, until adults figured out that she had absolutely no control over what it did. It normally took people time to realize that they wanted nothing to do with her.

The captain blinked, slowly. "I'm sorry?"

"You don't like me," said Zib. "*Why* don't you like me? I haven't done anything to make you not like me."

"You're doing something right now," said the captain.

"But that's not the way things work. You can't be mean to someone and then say them being mad at you for being mean justifies being mean in the first place. Time has to be a straight line or it stops meaning anything. Cause and, um, effect."

The captain frowned. "You are small and uneducated," she said. "Who are you to lecture me on cause and effect?"

Zib, as a storm cloud stitched into a little girl's body, had had plenty of opportunity to learn about causes and effects. Even before she'd been too young to fully understand them, she'd been learning about them, a lesson contained in every broken window and raised adult voice. Perhaps that was why she was able to square her shoulders, stand up straight, and look the captain in the eye as she said, "Whoever knows more gets to explain the thing. It doesn't matter how much older you are, or how much smarter you think you are, if you don't know the thing, you don't get to be the teacher."

The captain blinked again, this time in visible surprise. The edge of annoyance melted from her face as she studied Zib. "All right," she said. "I won't teach, then, and I'm sorry I tried. I don't like you because you're not of water, at all; you're of air if you're anything, and air children who come here are usually trying to spy for the Queen of Swords. She'll not make monsters of my crew if there's anything I can do to intervene."

"The Queen of Swords tried to have me, and I told her no," said Zib. "Where we come from, children don't belong to just one element. We're people, and I guess we have all the elements in us, but mostly we're made out of blood and bones and meat. So I'm not a child of air, whatever that means, and I'm not spying for anyone. I wish you'd said something before you just decided not to like me. I could have told you I wasn't hers a long time ago."

The captain sighed and shook her head. "If I'd straight-up told you, you might have said you weren't hers even though you were. Sometimes approaching things in the most straightforward way means that you can't get a real answer, only the answer people think you want to hear. I'm sorry you felt I didn't like you. It was never my intention to make you uncomfortable."

"But you did," said Zib.

"I did," agreed the captain. "That is why I am apologizing. But you are all members of my crew for right now, and a captain can't apologize too much to members of their crew without weakening their place, so I'm done saying I'm sorry to you. I made a bad assumption. I'll try not to do that again." She turned as if to walk away.

"Please wait," said Avery. "We still have something to ask you."

The captain glanced at him quizzically. "What did you need to ask me? She"—and she gestured to Zib—"said you had a question, and then she asked a question, and it was a big question, and I answered it."

"We have a different question." Avery shot a heatless glance over at Zib. He understood why she had asked what she had asked, and he couldn't blame her for needing to know. It was difficult to be disliked by an adult, especially when you hadn't done anything at all to earn that dislike. The captain had been kind to the rest of them and barely tolerant of Zib, and he would have asked why in her place. Some things stung too much to be ignored.

"All right," said the captain, with barely concealed impatience. "What do you want to ask me?"

"Who is the woman in the locked little room at the top of the stairs?"

The captain froze, absolutely and completely. For a moment, Avery wasn't even sure she was breathing. Then, stone-faced and low-voiced, she said, "No."

"But we've seen her and spoken to her," said Niamh. "She's very much there, and her stairway keeps appearing to us."

"So do not climb the stairs," said the captain. "She is not for you to speak with, or to speak of. She is a shadow, a story of the sea, and she should be left alone to fade away. Stories only vanish when they are forgotten."

Zib and Avery exchanged a glance, horrified. Neither of them wanted to vanish, or wanted to think about people they'd met, even if only briefly, vanishing. "But she's real," protested Zib. "We saw her! She told us her name! Shadows don't have names, they're just shadows!"

The captain took a step backward, away from them, into the full glare of the sunlight, and for the first time, Zib saw that she cast no shadow. She was a tall, imposing woman, but she might as well have been standing in darkness, for the light could coax no shade from her feet.

"Shadows are just shadows, and should be left alone," said the captain. "Only the ones who cast them have any right to say what they can and cannot do. Leave her alone. If you see the stairs again, do not climb them, but turn your backs and wait for them to disappear. This is an order from your captain. Now, all of you, find something that needs to be cleaned up. We need to get shipshape and ready to sail again."

She strode off across the deck, sailors scattering to get out of her way before she could turn her darkening temper in their direction, and into her cabin, slamming the door behind herself.

NINE

AFTER THE STORM

Storms are dangerous things, whether they happen on the land or out at sea. They can break down tree limbs and snap ropes, tear holes in sails, and scatter barrels and other essential supplies without regard for where they actually belong. The four children exchanged a look and scattered, doing as they'd been told, finding things on the deck that needed to be put to rights.

Zib swarmed up into the rigging with the sailors who were dedicated to retying all the knots and securing the loosened sails. Her hands were quick and clever, and in short order, she had done the work of three men, aided by her frustration and by her narrow, nimble fingers. She flipped around, hanging upside down from the rigging, and beamed at the sailors around her.

"All right," she said. "What else needs to be done?"

Niamh looked at the deck itself, where pools of seawater had been left by the lashing waves and crashing rain, smiled, and began to dance. It was a slow, swirling thing, and she raised her hands as she moved, and the water began to move with her. It collected from all corners of the deck, rolling together until it formed pools large enough to shape themselves into short humanoid figures, the tops of their heads barely coming up to her shoulder. The puddle-people began dancing with her, forming a complicated pattern of turns and spins. Niamh danced closer and closer to the rail, until, with deep, respectful bows, each of the puddle people slipped through the rail in turn, dropping into the sea without a sound. Niamh stopped dancing and stood on the perfectly dry deck, smiling to herself.

The sailors nearby stared for a moment before putting their mops down and moving on to other tasks. They knew better than to object to something that made their lives so much easier.

The Crow Girl couldn't fly or even burst into birds, but she was still a murder at heart, all black wings and clever claws and sharp eyes designed to spot things from the air. She began roving over the deck, pausing every few feet to pick up a nail or a grommet or a bit of ship's hardware that had been broken loose by the wind. She dug a belt buckle out of a crack in the wood. It was neither as showy as Niamh's water-ghosts or as daredevil as Zib's ascent into the rigging, but it was still profoundly useful, at least based on the grateful cry of the sailor into whose hands she tipped her treasures, smiling brightly at him before she scampered off to make another pass. The sailor promptly filled his pockets with metal bits, looking faintly astonished, and wandered off to transfer them to a more secure box.

Avery watched his friends as they got to work, feeling suddenly useless. He had been exactly what the captain needed when she wanted to have her books sorted, but out here, in the sun and the spray, he couldn't think of a single thing he could do to contribute. His hands were too soft for tying ropes or moving fallen timbers; the water was all gone, danced away by the drowned girl; there was no way he could find any other sparkling bits of metal on the deck, not with the Crow Girl's constantly scanning eyes fixed at her feet. So what could he do?

Hesitantly, he took a step toward the captain's cabin. No one rushed to stop him, and he took another, and another, moving more quickly with every step, until he was standing in front of the closed door. The books had already been falling from the steps when the storm had been young and he had been sent below with the others. Surely they must be scattered everywhere now, in dire need of some solemn, studious child to pick them up and put them away.

Carefully, he raised his hand and knocked on the cabin door. The sound of heavy footsteps answered almost immediately, and then, before his nerves could falter, the captain was opening the door, looking down at him with narrowed, disapproving eyes. Avery coughed, feeling his cheeks flush red and his chest get tight.

"You said to clean things up," he said, forcing the words up a suddenly dry throat and past his unbending lips. "I'm not good with a mop and I can't string a sail, but I can clean up the books that fell during the storm, if you'll let me come in."

"You were respectful enough of them before," she said, somewhat grudgingly, and stepped aside, letting him in.

As he had feared, the bookshelves were all but empty, their contents spread across the floor. The rugs were thick and soft enough to have blunted their fall, and it didn't look as if any of them had been damaged, but he still wanted to sweep them into his arms and reassure them that the worst was past and they would be all right now, no one was going to hurt them again. The captain watched him for a moment before retreating to her drafting table, picking up a compass, and returning to the work she had been doing before he interrupted her.

With all the books scattered across the floor, Avery was free to begin organizing them as he liked. He kept to the alphabet, naturally, but began "A" at floor-level, which had always seemed to him to be the most sensible way to approach a filing system. "B" was put next, the alphabet winding up the bookshelf like a large and literate snake that added its joints one letter at a time.

He worked in efficient silence until he had reached the letter "L," and his hand fell upon a book titled *Lore and Legends of the Saltwise Sea*. It was bound in blue silk, as rich and textured as the waves outside, and the weight of it was both more and less than it should have been possible for a single book to be. He hugged it to his chest, suddenly overcome with longing, and climbed to his feet in order to approach the captain. The rug muffled his footsteps, and so she didn't look up until he was almost beside her.

"Yes?" she asked.

"May I . . . may I borrow this? Please?" He turned the book shyly toward her, not quite willing to let it out of his hands. "Our cabin is nice, but it's very small, and very empty, and I'm used to a story before bed."

If it had been Zib asking, the captain's answer might well have been different, and she would have felt no shame over that. But this was Avery, sweet and shy and always very popular with adults. She tilted her head, and smiled a little, and said, "Certainly you may. But be very careful with it, for all my books are rare and precious to me, and I would not be pleased if any damage were to come to one of them."

Avery nodded and stepped back, still clutching the book to his chest. He knew a warning when he heard one: if he allowed this book to be harmed, he wouldn't be allowed to borrow any others. As he had yet to see any others he wished to borrow, this was perhaps less of a threat than it might have been, but she could also forbid him to play librarian for her, and lacking any other jobs on the ship that suited him, it was very important that he be allowed to do this one. He returned to the piles of books yet to be put away, keeping his precious book of legends close to hand, and went back to work.

There was too much mess to be unmade in a single session, but little enough that he was up to the letter R when the captain said, "The light is going. You should stop for now, or you'll begin making mistakes, and I'd prefer you only need to do the work once."

Avery looked up, startled. The cabin had no windows, but the light slipping through around the edges of the door was considerably dimmer than it had been, and the shadows forming around the oil lamps were considerably deeper. "Oh," he said, climbing to his feet again, snatching up the book as he did, so that he could clutch it hard against his chest. "All right. Are you coming to dinner?"

"I'll be there shortly," said the captain, and opened the door for him, so that he could step out onto the twilit deck.

Zib was still dangling from the rigging by one foot, laughing to herself like she was somehow doing the cleverest thing anyone had ever done. Niamh and the Crow Girl were standing by the rail with Jibson, chatting quietly. Avery walked over to them as the captain closed the door behind him, looking around.

The deck of the ship was sparkling clean, as if it had never been disheveled in the first place. The sails and riggings were tight and properly arrayed; the metal fixings had been returned to the bits of rail and structural flashing that had lost them; everything that had been tipped over or toppled had been tidily restored. Jibson smiled at Avery's approach.

"Been working for the captain, eh, lad? What have you got there?"

"A book," said Avery, who had never cared for being talked to like he was a child, even though he had been a child every day of his life so far, save for the ones where he had been a baby. "I borrowed it from the captain, with her permission."

There was a clatter of metal on wood as Zib dropped down from the rigging and landed on her iron-shod feet. She came trotting over to the group. "Are you going to read us a story tonight, Avery?" she asked, without any of the teasing he would have expected from one of the girls at school asking the same question.

Avery nodded, tilting the book so Zib could see the title. "It's about stories of the sea."

"Oh!" said Zib, eyes going wide and round. Then she nodded, vigorously. "That sounds like a good story. It's almost time for dinner, although I don't really understand how it can be when Maddy said she serves twice a day, and we already had eggs and sandwiches."

"She also said there would be bread and cheese in

the middle of the day, and lunch was grilled cheese sandwiches," said Niamh. "Maybe she meant it when she said she could always feed hungry children."

Jibson laughed. "You've already figured Maddy out, missy. She doesn't do anything proper complicated for lunch, but with your friend with the hungry hair helping her with the morning dishes, and the four of you being so young, she made an extra effort today. I'm sure she'll do that a time or two more, as long as she keeps getting help."

Zib, who could see the future stretching out in front of her in a line of dishwater basins, swallowed a groan and turned toward the door. If there was dinner in the offing, she wanted to be there before the best bits of whatever it was had been taken by the rest of the crew.

She was far enough ahead that she was the first of their group to reach the mess, which was fuller than she had ever seen it, packed from wall to wall with pirates, all of them carousing, hefting mugs that didn't look like they contained orange juice this time, and eating noisily from large bowls filled with what appeared to be some sort of meaty stew. Maddy was in her customary place, dishing up bowls and hunks of rough bread to the sailors who approached her. She smiled at the sight of the children, waving for them to approach.

Again, Zib was the first there, beaming as Maddy pushed a bowl of stew and a heel of bread into her hands. "Are you coming to help with the breakfast dishes again tomorrow?" she asked hopefully. "That was more of a help than you could possibly have known it would be, and I promise not to keep you forever, I know young things need to be moving around whenever they can be."

"I will," said Zib, almost before she had realized she was going to speak. She smiled and grimaced at the same time, creating an entirely new expression that was not, it must be said, a wholly pleasant one. "It's only a few hours, and if you have help, we get lunch, right? I don't mind."

"But you do mind, and that makes it all the kinder," said Maddy. "It's an easy thing to do a job you fancy. To do a job that tasks you so is a great gift to the person you work with, and I'll do my best to be worthy of it. Now all of you, off to eat. Grab a pitcher of bonberry juice as you go. You won't like what the sailors are drinking."

"Yes, ma'am," said Zib, and picked up a pitcher before heading for the nearest open table. The others were close behind her. Niamh sniffed her stew as she sat.

"Chicken and root vegetables," she said. "No fish. Again. I don't think I've seen a single scale since we came onboard."

"The captain said their nets keep coming back empty," said the Crow Girl. "They can't catch anything, so they can't serve anything. That only makes sense."

"But why can't they catch anything?" asked Zib. "It's a big ocean, and they have big, big nets. I patched holes in a couple of them today. There's no reason for them not to be able to catch more fish than they can eat, unless the Saltwise Sea doesn't have any fish in it?"

Niamh shook her head. "No, the Saltwise Sea is full of fish. Funny-looking ones, all different colors, with fins like veils, or with so many teeth that they could eat you up in just two bites. Sometimes they would get swept into the frozen city by the currents, coming up under the ice and looking for a way home again. We made one of them our mayor for a whole season, until the ice broke enough that he could find his way back to the ocean. He was an excellent mayor. He only ate two councilors, and most people agreed that both of them very much deserved it."

The children were silent for a moment, considering the idea of a world where a fish could serve as mayor and devour anyone who frustrated them. Zib poured out cups of bonberry juice, which was sweet and sour at the same time, and kept eating her stew. She had long since learned the value of eating when there was food in front of you, and didn't consider any question or mystery to be worth the possibility of missing a meal.

Avery held up the book he'd borrowed from the captain. "Maybe this can tell us more about the woman at the top of the stairs," he said. "It can't hurt to look."

"Why do people always say that?" asked the Crow Girl. "I looked at the Page of Frozen Waters while she was sorting her weapons, once, and when she spotted me, it hurt plenty. She said I was spying, but I wasn't spying, I was looking, and they're not the same thing, or they'd have the same name. She didn't have to hurt me."

Jibson plunked down onto the bench next to her, causing her to squawk in brief surprise. His bowl was only half-full, and the pitcher in his hand was distinctly not bonberry juice. "Looking and spying feel the same to the person doing them. It's the person they're being done *to* who gets to decide which is which. You've met the Page of Frozen Waters, then?"

"We all have," said Niamh. "We'd prefer not to do it again."

"But we will," said the Crow Girl. "She's never going to forgive us for getting away from her."

Jibson nodded slowly. "Some people are like that," he said.

"I don't think she's people," said Avery. "A blizzard isn't people. A bad storm isn't people. The Page of Frozen Waters is more like those things than she is like a people."

"We can't decide who is and isn't people, even when we think we should be able to," said Jibson. "I've met a lot of people where it would have been easier to pretend that they weren't, but all the pretending there is wouldn't have changed what they were. As long as someone's still people, you have to treat them with kindness."

"You're a pirate," said the Crow Girl. "What do you know about treating people with kindness?"

Jibson looked at her sadly. "I know that most of us would rather still be sailing with the navy, like we were before the King destroyed the Lady and took up with that Page. We don't want to hurt anyone. We steal because starving for your principles is still starving, and none of us are so loyal that we want to die for loyalty, but we've never hurt anyone on purpose. Being pirates didn't turn us cruel. If it had, I think this ship would have far fewer sailors by now, as we'd have been deserting since the day we understood what we'd done to ourselves."

"But you don't desert," blurted Avery.

"No, we don't," said Jibson. "We love our captain, for all that she can't love us, and we stay in the hopes that one day she'll remember how to let her heart come home." He took the last bite of his stew and stood. "Goodnight, children. Sleep well when it comes to that."

"We will," said Zib. She resumed shoveling stew into her mouth. She hadn't thought she would be hungry, not after the size of lunch, but climbing took energy, and tying seemingly endless knots had been more difficult than she'd expected. She ate every bite of her stew and every crumb of her bread, which was brown and heavy and surprisingly soft, like the bread her grandmother baked. She wished she had a pat of butter to melt into it, all golden sweetness dripping on her fingers, but even unbuttered, it was delicious.

Niamh finished about the same time Zib did. Zib bounced to her feet, grabbing the other girl's bowl, and carried both over to the waiting basin, where she shared a quick smile with Maddy before returning to the table. The Crow Girl was just finishing her own meal, and Zib took her bowl as well, dropping it in the basin before looking meaningfully at Avery. He wasn't dawdling, precisely, but was eating with slow, thoughtful bites, taking his time and savoring the meal. He glanced up, meeting Zib's eyes, and swallowed hard before he started eating faster, not quite gulping his food.

"Bowl," said Zib, holding out her hand imperiously. Avery sighed and plopped it into her palm, a few bites of stew still sitting lonely at the bottom. Zib whisked it away as he stood, gathering the book once more against his chest.

"I guess it's time for bed and stories," he said. "Come on."

The Crow Girl and Niamh were quick to fall into step behind him. Zib joined the group as they were reaching the door, and together the four of them returned to the cabin they had been assigned. Without a word, they removed their iron shoes and tumbled into their bunks, getting comfortable and settling in for the story ahead.

Avery propped himself up against his pillow and opened the book to the table of contents. Now, a table of contents is a very important thing. It tells what can be found where in a text, and when that text is unfamiliar, that can be essential. "The Story of the Maiden and the Seven Pearls," he read. "Jack the Clever Is Beset by Swans. The Fallen Lighthouse. Where the Sea Dragon Keeps His Heart. The Lady of Salt and Sorrow."

"Oh, read that one," cried Niamh, interrupting him. "She's the patron of my city, and we haven't seen her in ever so long, not since the King of Cups took up with the Page of Frozen Waters and stripped her of her crown."

"You said you couldn't find her bones," said Zib, with bloodthirsty curiosity. "Does that mean you think she's dead?"

"It means we know she loves us, and would never have stayed away for this long if she had any choice at all," said Niamh. "She could be dead. I wouldn't put it past him to have killed her. But if that book has her story in it, I want to hear it."

"All right," said Avery, and flipped ahead in the book to the story she had requested. He took a deep breath, and read, "Long ago and far away, when summer tides were kinder . . ."

TEN

THE LADY OF SALT AND SORROW

"... there lived a drowned girl from the city of eternal winters. She was very cold, always, for she had drowned when she was but an infant, falling out of her father's fishing boat and into the water without even the opportunity to scream. Her swaddling clothes had been enough to drag her down to the bottom, and though her family had searched for many days, they had never been able to find her body. Only when their boats were brought back to shore and her weeping mother had been led away had the people of the city beneath the ice come for her, gathering her from the lakebed and carrying her away to their watery streets and the frigid, frozen walls of their palace.

"There are cities underwater inhabited by nymphs

and naiads and merpeople of all kinds, but the cities of the drowned are not like them. Everyone who lives there—and they do live, in their cold, breathless way—is someone who fell from the dry world and drowned, lungs and throat full of choking water, the slowing of their heart the transfer of their citizenship. Because of this, they cannot have children of their own, for their bodies have forgotten the means of making life out of nothing. When a family in a drowned city desires a child, they must tell the queen, and she will keep watch for drowned children, assigning them as best fits the needs of her people.

"When this babe drowned, however, the queen herself was ready to expand her family, to take an heir from the dry world to raise as her own. An infant was the best possible choice for her, for although she could see the terrible tragedy of the drowned babe's existence, her people would most easily accept an heir who had been brought up entirely in their ways, who would never be tempted to leave the water and go looking for the family that had borne her. So when the guards carried the baby into the palace, the queen greeted them with wide-spread arms and a joyous cry of 'My daughter! My daughter! You found my daughter!'

"So the guards placed the girl in their queen's arms, and if a few of them felt some small pangs of regret, that they had not been afforded the opportunity to name the child as their own, they were all clever enough to keep quiet. The queen took the girl to her private chambers, and when she emerged with her a fortnight later, all traces of the dry world had been wiped quite thoroughly away. The girl gurgled and laughed and breathed the water as naturally as any other drowned child, and the people filled the streets in joyous celebration, for they had a princess now, and they had already decided they would love her."

"Is that really how babies are made where you come from?" blurted Zib.

"It is," said Niamh. "We grow up very slowly, under the ice, and the cold keeps us children for as long as we wish to be. I was born in Crocus, according to the guards who found me, and I drowned when I was too small to swim. Not too small to have wandered into the edge of the lake and been swept away by one of the deep currents, no, but too small to swim all the same. I don't remember the family I had before I drowned and was reborn. They may have thrown me to the lake on purpose. It happens. When there isn't enough food and there are too many mouths to feed, some people will give their children to the lake for safekeeping. They know we'll wake and live again. But I like to believe they mourned me. We always like to believe that, when we can."

Avery took a breath and resumed reading: "The queen named the girl Seiche, after the greatest of the lake-bound storms, and raised her in peace and plenty in the palace. Seiche was so sweet and so beloved of all who knew her that tales of her grace and beauty spread through all the drowned lands. She knew that her mother needed an heir who could hold the throne, and so she did not linger over childhood, as so many drowned children choose to do, but progressed through it at the ordinary speed, counting her birthday from the day of her drowning. And so it was that on her sixteenth birthday she stood before her mother's people and claimed them as her own people, promising to do her duty if it was ever required of her.

"That night, there was a visitor at the palace gates. Drowned lands get few guests. Most of those who would travel to see their splendor are unable to breathe below the water, but this man had no such trouble. He was tall and slim as the blade of a knife, with a crown upon his brow, and the palace guards opened the doors for him, for they knew that the King of Cups could go where he liked beneath the water."

"Even though it wasn't his kingdom?" asked Zib. "It seems to me the queen should have been able to tell him no if she wanted to, since it wasn't his kingdom."

"But it was," said the Crow Girl. "The drowned lands are all underwater, and so they belong to the King of Cups first and forever. He can come and go as he likes when he does it below the water. The palace guards did the right thing by letting him in. Anything else would have been denying him his protectorate, and then he would have been justified in summoning tempests that would grind them into river rocks and flecks of ice. The drowned always belong to him, for they carry the water in their skins and in their souls."

"She's right," said Niamh. "It's why I'm always damp. The water wanders with me. Even if I can't go home, I'm still drowned."

"Oh," said Zib, eyes going wide and round with the complexity of it all. It seemed like such a strange rule to her, who came from a world where people could be dried off with a towel, and a king was a king, not the beginning of a progression of smaller kings, all nestled inside each other like nesting dolls.

Avery coughed and returned his attention to the book, reading, "The guards allowed the King of Cups to enter, but the youngest and wariest of them broke from her position and ran to find the queen, who was in her chambers. She did not knock when she reached the doors, but burst inside, against all her training and all of royal law.

"The queen, seated at her dressing table, looked up in shocked surprise, for no one had dared to burst in on her in a very long time. She saw that the guard was young. She saw that the guard was frightened, pale and shaking, with ice crystals forming in her tangled hair. Many among the drowned grow colder when they are afraid, even as those who walk in the sunlight may find their skin becoming hot with the frenzied fever of their blood. It is through such small things that we know the drowned are not merely another form of our dead, but a new people altogether, for all that we share a common origin."

Zib looked to Niamh, who nodded, confirming the story, and hugged her knees to her chest as she continued to listen.

"The queen was not known for her temper, or for her cruelty. So she rose from her seat and went to the guard, embracing her in all her frightened coldness. 'What is wrong, my dear?' she asked. 'Why are you here in such disarray?'

"'The King of Cups is come,' gasped the guard. 'He appeared at the gate as if he had every right to be here, and he is dressed as a man gone courting. I fear he comes for the princess. It can be no coincidence that he arrived the night following her majority.'

"The queen listened to these words and knew them for the truth they were, for the King of Cups did nothing without good cause. She took her crown from its place on the dressing table and lowered it to her head, where it rested as if it had been made for her and there had never been nor would ever be another queen beneath the ice. 'Rest here, and know that you are my most favored,' she said to the guard. 'I will go to receive our king.'

"She walked the halls of her palace with neither guard nor escort, head up and shoulders back, and when she came to her throne room the King of Cups was already there, smiling at the Princess Seiche, her small hand obscured by his large ones. And the princess was smiling back at him, eyes bright as sunlight on the water, and the queen knew she was too late after all. She had waited so long for a child and heir, and now that wait would begin anew, for the King of Cups looked at Seiche as a child may look at a cake, all hunger and wanting and no concern at all for what someone else might desire."

Avery paused, frowning at the book. "That doesn't make any sense. If she'd already pledged to be a princess for her people, why would she go off with the King of Cups? He's not a nice man. I wouldn't go off with him."

"He was a nice man, once," said the Crow Girl, haltingly. "Before he lost the Lady of Salt and Sorrow, before he shared his court with the Page of Frozen Waters. I don't think her story will be in that book. She's not a drowned girl, not like Niamh or Seiche in the story. She's a frozen maiden, and they're different, and they're terrible. She'd freeze the world if she could have the way of it, and leave us all encased in ice and unable to escape from whatever terrible thing she plans to do next. But before his heart was frozen, before he lost the knack of caring about the people around him, yes, the King of Cups was kinder. It's no real surprise that a princess would fall in love with him."

Avery looked unsure, as if this explanation left out too many pieces for him to be entirely comfortable with it. But he turned back to the book, and read, "The King of Cups led Seiche to the sea, which she had never seen before, and built for her a cottage on the shore, where she could watch the wind and the waves, and where the water would carry messages between her and her mother if she wished it to. And he came to her often, and they were lovers by the side of the sea, and they thought nothing would ever change again, for they had each other, and they were happy."

"Ew," said Zib. "Mushy stuff."

"Mushy and weird," said Avery. "What changed?"

"The Page of Frozen Waters," said Niamh. "She changed everything. She's a monster, and not of his making. He had no defenses against her."

"Oh," said Avery, and read, "The people of the Saltwise Sea called Seiche the Lady of Salt and Sorrow, for she was theirs, and she mourned her mother and her home, for all that she had left willingly. Not all hearts are broken without cause. She was good to them, and they loved her, more even than the King of Cups did, for he had other lands to tend over, and she was always by their side. They made of her a story of the sea, well-loved and oft-recited, the sort of tale meant to be told when the wind blows cold and the sky burns red. She was born, she drowned, she was beautiful, she disappeared. On such foundations are legends all too often built. Now rest my dears, and be at ease; there's a fire in the hearth and a wind in the eaves. And the night is so dark and the dark is so deep, and it's time that all good little stars were asleep." He turned the page and scowled, clearly frustrated. "That's where it ends. That wasn't a story at all! That was just pieces of a story. Where did she go? Did she ever find her family again? How did the Page get the attention of the King?" For it was difficult to think of the sleepy, sullen man they had all met as the sort of figure who could win the heart of a princess.

"I don't know any of those answers except for one," said Zib. "I think she's on this ship. Lýpi said that she's a story of the sea, and the captain doesn't want us letting her out."

"Fairy stories aren't real," said Avery.

"What you call fairy stories, we call history," said the Crow Girl. "Put the book down. Get some sleep. Tomorrow is going to be complicated."

"Life so often is," said Niamh, and blew her lantern out.

ELEVEN

ROCKED AWAY

There were no windows in the cabin; Avery knew it was morning by the sound of Zib climbing the bunks, and her hushed giggles as she shook the Crow Girl awake. The Crow Girl grumbled but didn't burst into birds, which seemed to be as close as she could come to acquiescence. Niamh slid out of her own bed, damp feet squelching against the floor, and picked up her iron shoes before leaning over Avery. Water dripped off her hair to splatter on his cheek. He wiped it roughly away, rolling over and away from her. She leaned further over the bunk, and water splattered on his opposite cheek. Avery opened his eyes, turning his head enough to glare at her.

Niamh smiled, all in innocence. "Oh, good," she

said. "You're awake. I was starting to worry you might sleep the entire day away."

"How could you *tell*?" He sat up, rubbing his face dry with his hands. "I don't know what time it is. There's no way you can tell the time. The sun can't find us here."

"The tide," she said simply. "I feel it turn. When I'm this close to the water, I always know what time it is, and right now, the tide says that it's time for you to get out of bed, you old lazybones. Don't you want to talk to the captain?"

It all came back in a rush. The borrowed book, the story that didn't finish itself, the strange woman in the locked room, and the questions they were intending to ask the captain. Avery found himself gripped with the sudden urge to stuff his head under the pillow and shut out the rest of the world—especially the three girls who were now shuffling through their own attempts at getting ready for the day.

"I want a bath," said Zib. "I don't think I've ever said that before, but that doesn't make it be not true. I want a bath, and I want clean clothes, and I want to brush my hair."

Her hair, which had been resembling a hydra more and more as time went by, seemed to silently agree. It was less tangled than terrifying, as if it had decided to aspire to become a blackberry bramble and begin abducting children. *Could* they be abducted at this point, with their parents in a different country and entirely unable to come to their defense? The thought was a frightening one. Avery set it steadfastly aside as he finally sat up and slid out of the bunk.

"Maybe there's someplace to take a bath here on the ship," he said. "We can ask the captain."

"We have better things to ask the captain," said Zib. "We need to know if the woman in the cage is the Lady of Salt and Sorrow."

"So what if she is?" asked Avery. "We don't know why she's locked up."

"If we let her out, maybe the King will stop being a bad guy," said Zib. "I don't want him to find us. I don't want to go back in his cage while he coaxes feathers out of my bones."

"He's not the one we need to be afraid of," said Niamh. "The Page will hunt us down long before he does."

"And if we bring back the Lady, maybe the Page goes away," said Zib.

The Crow Girl shrugged. "It's as good a guess as any," she said. "I don't really understand how it works with the nobility. They keep their practice and their power to themselves, and vermin like me stand to the outside and hope they don't get close enough to decide that we're worth the effort of hurting."

Avery nodded and stepped into his iron shoes. "Can you be birds yet?"

The Crow Girl shook her head, expression turning mournful. "Still no," she said. "I should be scared, but my heart's beating better now that it's remembering what it means to be only one heart and not a hundred. I think maybe I've been birds too much, and I need to be a girl for a while. But I don't know why I can't be birds at all."

"You lost the favor of the King of Cups when you left him, and we're surrounded all the way by water," said Niamh. "I wouldn't be surprised if he's withholding his gifts from you as a punishment."

"Any gift you can take away that easily was never a gift at all," said the Crow Girl, in an oddly philosophical tone. Avery realized that she had been sounding less scattered, less distractible, since she had donned her iron shoes and stopped trying to fly away. Maybe there was more to becoming birds than he'd originally assumed. Maybe she'd been getting lost within the murder, and needed to remember how to be a person rather than a collective. It was a chilling thought. Even here in the Up-and-Under, where water could have opinions and people could be seasons, there was a cost for the things people might want to give you.

Nothing came for free.

"All right," said Avery. "Let's go see the captain."

As if on cue, Zib's stomach gave a growl so loud it was audible several feet away, and she pressed her hands against it, like it was a wild animal she was trying to contain. "Food first?" she asked pleadingly. "It's breakfast time, and Maddy will miss us if we don't come for something to eat. And some orange juice. Orange juice is important when you're out at sea."

"I guess we can stop for something to eat," said Avery, his own stomach rumbling at the thought. He wasn't starving, but what they were about to say to the captain might upset her enough that she decided to stop letting them have anything they thought of as nice. He'd heard stories from an uncle who'd been a member of the Navy for a while, and apparently, most people who went sailing lived on salted pork and something called "hardtack," which didn't sound appealing in the slightest.

"Yay!" said Zib, and hugged him quickly, her hair slapping him across the face and catching in his mouth before she ran out of her room, steps surprisingly nimble for all that she was wearing iron shoes.

The trip to the mess hall was easy, following what was fast becoming a familiar path. Several sailors were already there, attention fixed on their own meals, as was Maddy, who served them oatmeal with brown sugar and sliced-up peaches, smiling a sly smile when the Crow Girl asked where all the fresh fruit had come from. The children gathered together at the table where they had settled the day before, eating almost too fast to taste their food, gulping down cups of orange juice like liquid sunshine, like the power of the sky transmuted into the sweetness that lingered on the backs of their tongues, like a promise.

When they finished, it was Zib who gathered up their bowls and spoons and whisked them away to the basin, where she paused long enough to have a quickly murmured conversation with Maddy before bounding back over to the others and grabbing Avery by the arm, as if she thought she could, through sheer force of will, force him to start moving at her speed.

"Well?" she chirped. "Come on, come on, we have questions to ask and stories to hear and doors to open, and we're not doing any of those things sitting here with our chins in our hands. We have to move!"

Avery, who had long since figured out that Zib was a force of nature, and that sometimes it was genuinely better to give in and let himself be swept away, stood. Niamh and the Crow Girl did the same, and together the four children left the mess hall and made their way up to the deck.

There had been no storms in the night. Sails which had been tightly tied when they went to bed were still tightly tied now; rails which had been buffed smooth and clean were still polished to pointed perfection. Sailors moved through the open space, adjusting ropes, checking knots, and generally keeping them sailing onward. The captain was nowhere to be seen.

Avery, who was by this point relatively comfortable approaching the captain's cabin, led the rest of them across the deck and raised his hand to knock, twice. A moment later, the door swung open, revealing the captain herself, still blinking and bleary with sleep.

"What is it?" she demanded.

"I read that book you let me borrow," Avery said. "And we had a question for you."

"About a book of fairy tales?" asked the captain.

She had little enough experience with children that she didn't recognize the danger in children with questions about fairy tales. Fairy tales are lies wrapped around kernels of truth, meant to make the world comprehensible and clear. When they are questioned, it is almost always because the one asking the questions has found a crack in the lies and is homing in on something that, perhaps, they were not yet meant to understand.

"Yes," said Niamh. "There are stories of my city in that book. The city under the ice."

"How are you here if you come from there?" asked the captain.

"There was a thaw," said Niamh. "I surfaced to see the world where I had been born before my drowning, and while I was on the shore, the lake froze again. I can't go home until the next thaw, which could be tomorrow, or could be never. I walk in the world of the air-breathers until such time as the ice allows."

"Hmmm," said the captain. "Perhaps next time, you'll know better."

"Perhaps," said Niamh.

"Seiche," said Zib. The captain whipped around to stare at her, eyes going wide and glossy. "The Lady of Salt and Sorrow. She comes from Niamh's city."

"She did," said the captain slowly.

"Is she locked in that little room?" The question was asked with solemn innocence, as if Zib couldn't imagine a world where an honest answer wasn't given.

"We don't speak her name on this ship," said the

captain. "Not the name she had before she left the King. The wind has ears, and it's impossible to sail entirely free of the Queen of Swords. Perhaps that's why the Queen of Wands was the one to go missing; it's possible to sail beyond the reach of fire, but not of wind. Quiet."

"But we have questions," said Avery.

"Having them doesn't have to mean asking them. I don't want to hear whatever questions you might have."

"Why are you afraid of the wind?" asked Zib.

The captain's face darkened, like clouds rolling across a previously sunlit sky. She took a step backward into her cabin, beckoning the children to follow her inside. Only once the last of them was past the threshold did she close the door and ask, "Have you met the Queen of Swords?"

"Of course I have," said the Crow Girl. "She makes monsters. She made me."

"Do you remember what that means?"

"I—" The Crow Girl paused, her face falling. "No. I traded my name for my wings, and a name is a big thing to give away. It carries so much of who you are and who you were, all wrapped up in however many letters, and without it, those things are lost as well. I'm not who I was before I became a monster. I won't ever be that person again, not unless we have my name back from her, and I'd have to give my wings away for that, so it's not going to happen."

"It means she ripped out your heart and replaced

it with a black-winged bird," said the captain grimly. "She can do almost anything, if it's allowed. The knives of the wind are the sharpest of all. They flense skin from flesh and flesh from bone when they blow. Her winds blow even here, and if she hears the Lady's name, she may turn her terrible gaze in our direction. Her Page is not so fearsome as the King of Cups's, but he's frightening enough, if you don't have any way to block him out."

"Do *all* the Kings and Queens have scary Pages?" asked Zib.

"There are many pages in a story," said the captain implacably. "The Queen of Wands is served by the Page of Gentle Embers, who is a kind soul, and hardly ever burns anything important into ash, and the King of Coins is served by the Page of Smelted Silver, who is much more concerned with the making of money than he is with the breaking of hearts. Only Swords and Cups are truly terrifying."

"We've met the Page of Frozen Waters," said Avery. "Who serves the Queen of Swords?"

There was a rumble from outside, as if a terrible storm was upon them. The ship shook in the water, buffeted by a sudden howling wind. The captain grimaced. "The Page of Ceaseless Storms," she said. "He swings the wind like a whip, and stirs up all manner of terrible things. I have to go. They'll need me on the deck."

She turned for the door then, pausing only to say, "You should stay in here until the storm passes. He loses interest quickly when no one is attracting his attention."

Then she was gone, out into the gale, and the four children were left alone.

The ship shook and rocked and leapt in the water, sending books cascading to the floor. Avery made a small, shouted sound of dismay, moving toward them, and stopped as he saw Zib hurling herself at the door. "Where are you going?" he demanded.

"To help the captain!" she said, and opened the door, and was gone, out into the howling maelstrom of the storm.

The Crow Girl squawked and ran after her, and Niamh was close behind, both of them vanishing into the rain. Avery hesitated. It was warm and dry inside. It was safe inside. They were his friends, yes, but did friendship really demand that he endanger himself for the sake of the people who shared it? The Crow Girl was a survivor, and Niamh had already drowned; she wouldn't die the same way a second time.

Zib, on the other hand, was an ordinary little girl from his own ordinary town. She could drown. She could be blown away. One sword with barnacles on the hilt wasn't going to save her if something as terrible and inhuman as the Page of Frozen Waters—and he had to assume that the Page of Ceaseless Storms was of the same unspeakable breed—decided to have its way with her. Swallowing his own fears and protests, Avery ran for the door and plunged after the others, out into the storm.

Outside on the deck, the wind howled so loudly that it became a roar, a monster in its own right. The rain lashed down in sheets, turning the day into midnight's darkness. Try as he might, he couldn't see more than a few feet in any direction. "Zib!" he shouted, and the wind ripped his words away.

Avery spun in a circle, suddenly very aware that while everything he had told himself to get the courage to follow his friends outside was unquestionably true, he was also an ordinary kid from an ordinary town. He couldn't breathe water or break into birds and fly away; he didn't even have Zib's sword.

He was still trying to stop himself from panicking over the ordinariness of it all when there was a thump in front of him, so close that it was audible despite the wind. He looked in that direction, and paled as he saw a gray-skinned, white-haired child of about his own age balancing lightly on the deck, a trident in one hand.

"Hello," said the child, and somehow his voice was perfectly audible above the wind. "Are you the one who was yelling for the Lady of Salt and Sorrow?"

"No," whispered Avery. "Are you the Page of Ceaseless Storms?"

"I am!" said the child proudly. "The Queen of Swords has me listening for *that* name, because as long as the Lady is gone, the King of Cups is too busy dozing and dreaming and waiting for her to come home to challenge for more territory. It's better when they don't fight, so it's better that the Lady stay gone. I'm to watch for signs of her, and strike her down if she appears."

"My friends," said Avery. "They came out here to face you. Please, where are they? One was a Crow Girl, and one was a drowned girl, and one was a girl like me, with a sword in her hand and a whole summer tied up and captive in her hair."

"Oh," said the Page dismissively. "They've gone over the side. I can send you after them, if you would like. I'm sure they're still floating somewhere close enough to the surface for you to find."

Avery opened his mouth to protest, but it was too late; the Page waved his hand and the wind slammed into Avery's chest like a hammer slams into an anvil, and then he was falling, over the rail and tumbling along the length of the hull toward the waiting, hungry sea.

TWELVE

PIECES OF A PERSON

Avery hadn't been aware, before he struck the waves, that water could be a sort of stone; that it could be just as rigid and unyielding as anything else. The only mystery was how it could be rigid and unyielding, and fluid and shifting at the same time. The waves danced around him even as they dragged him down, and his lungs were empty and aching, and the contradiction didn't really matter, because he was going to drown.

He forced his eyes to stay open despite the stinging of the salt all around him, scanning the dark water for signs that he wasn't alone. At first, he couldn't find any. Then he saw a flicker of white at the very edge of his vision, and Niamh came swimming toward him. Her hair floated around her in a vast cloud, as did the white folds of her dress; her iron shoes were gone, probably knocked off her feet by the impact. He thrashed in the water, doing his best to swim toward her, but had made virtually no progress before she was upon him, looping her arm around his waist and hauling him toward the turbulent surface.

Avery spat and sputtered when she pulled him back into the air, trying to catch his breath. Niamh did no such thing, continuing to breathe as easily as if she hadn't just been submerged. Spitting out a last mouthful of salt, he demanded, "Where is Zib?"

Niamh shook her head. "We didn't fall together," she said. "The Crow Girl caught herself in a net hanging from the side of the ship before she hit the water, but Zib and I both fell all the way."

Avery looked up, and sure enough, there was the black blotch of the Crow Girl dangling from a sheet of netting, iron shoes still on her feet and hands clutching at the weave. She waved when she saw him, so tangled that this did nothing to change her position.

"Oh," he said, and pulled away from Niamh, doing his best to tread water unassisted. "We have to find her!"

"Can she swim?"

Avery didn't know. There was so much he didn't know about Zib, thanks to geography and parental opinions about what kinds of friends they should associate with keeping them from growing up with their hands in each other's pockets, as they maybe should have done. He shook his head, and Niamh dove again, leaving him alone.

There was a whistling sound overhead, cutting through the roaring of the wind. He looked up, and saw the small figure of the Page of Ceaseless Storms standing on the ship's rail. The Page saw him as well, and tipped his head in a mocking nod before stepping out onto the air, or rather, onto the lashing tendrils of the wind itself. He did not fall, but walked as confidently as if he were on solid ground. He dwindled with each step, becoming smaller and smaller, until he was entirely gone.

The storm followed after him, the winds quieting and the rain tapering off, although the waves, whipped to a frenzy as they were, continued their churning. Avery looked around again, splashing, frantic to find Zib.

It was the Crow Girl's startled squawk that caught his attention. Avery looked up again. The captain was standing on the rail, the woman from the locked room beside her. They were holding hands, fingers woven together like the strands of the net that held the Crow Girl. Together, they stepped off the edge and fell, plummeted, to the waiting, welcoming sea.

The water seemed to pull back as they fell toward it, creating a hole for them to tumble into. It closed again over their heads, and they were gone, leaving Avery alone. He struggled to stay afloat.

Zib was gone. Niamh was gone. Now even the

captain and her prisoner were gone, and he had no idea how he was going to get back onto the deck. He was going to drown here, cold and wet and miserable and lonely, and his parents would never know what had happened to him. Somehow, that was the worst part of all, that his parents should spend the rest of their lives waiting for the door to open and him to come walking back in, a little late from school but otherwise none the worse for wear. He was never going to see his father smile again, or ask his mother for an extra piece of toast. (And there was something wrong with that thought, that his sorrow over his father should be tied to what Avery could do to make *him* happy, while his sorrow over his mother should be tied to what she could do to make *Avery* happy, but he was on the edge of drowning, and didn't have time to question his own mind . . .)

A column of water rose out of the sea, and standing atop it was a woman he both knew and did not know, with Zib cradled, motionless in her arms. This woman was tall, with broad shoulders and strong legs and hair the color of seafoam, white and gray and endlessly tangled. Her face was beautiful, if not especially kind; warmth seemed to be something unfamiliar to her. She looked something like Niamh, with a certain essential dampness to her form, like she belonged at the bottom of the ocean.

The column shortened beneath her, until she was standing directly in front of him, somehow balanced on the waves themselves. Avery sputtered and thrashed in his efforts to keep from going under; she lifted a hand, and the water beneath him slowly became as solid as stone, until he was sitting on dry ground.

"I believe this is yours," she said, in a voice like the crashing of waves against the shore, and held Zib out to him.

Avery gathered the girl into his arms as best as he could, receiving a mouthful of wet, salty hair for his troubles, and asked, "Who are you?"

"I am who I was before I was someone I was not, and my name is best unspoken in the open air," said the woman.

Niamh surfaced next to Avery's feet, and gasped at the sight of the woman atop the water. "My . . . my lady!"

"Not any longer, but once," said the woman, and bent to offer a hand to Niamh, to pull her up onto the hardened water next to Avery. "My lord has taken another into his confidence, and left no space by his side for me. I have been hiding, split into my two aspects—a woman of salt and a woman of sorrow—to keep myself unseen. But neither salt nor sorrow can allow children to die without cause. I suppose I am revealed now, and all my revels to be ended."

In Avery's arms, Zib stirred and coughed, water spilling from her lips. The Lady sighed.

"Wake, child," she said, and Zib opened her eyes, sitting upright and striking Avery in the face with her hair once again. The Lady laughed. It was the sweetest sound any of them had ever heard.

"But . . . you could have come home," said Niamh.

"The ice, when frozen for one, is frozen for all," said the Lady. "If you are an exile, I am an exile as well, and nothing to be done for it. But take heart, child of my city: while we both live, the door may yet swing open once again."

"Now that you're yourself, and not two people, will you go to the King of Cups?" asked Avery.

"I could challenge his Page," said the Lady. "But the Queen of Swords might stop me, and I lack the strength to set myself against entire Courts. I had no intention of coming back together this soon."

"We're glad you did," said Avery. "Thank you."

Zib's iron shoes were still on her feet. They clinked dully on the hardened water as she shifted herself out of Avery's arms and stood. Above them in the netting, the Crow Girl burst into birds, and circled their heads before landing on their arms and shoulders. Zib laughed, bright and glorious and gay as anything.

The Lady smiled. "I am sorry to have confined your friend to a single shape before. To keep myself from reuniting, I had to block all magical reunion. Now that I am in one piece, she can be in as many as she likes."

"Magic is confusing," said Avery.

"Much of it is sympathetic; telling a thing that because it is similar to something else, they are the same. Usually, that improves the world. Sometimes, however, it casts barriers where none would otherwise have been."

Zib looked down, and gasped. Once the Crow Girl had joined them, and the four children were together once again, the hardened water beneath their feet had begun to gleam with a glittering, pearlescent light. "The improbable road!" she said, for indeed, that rare and fickle passage had found them once again.

The Lady looked down as well, and smiled. "I suppose your time on my ship is ended," she said. "If the road has come to claim you, you must go with it, or you could lose it forever."

"But we're wet," said Avery.

"You're walking on the sea," said the Lady.

"Come *on,* Avery," said Zib, and took a few steps away, following the gleam. The water continued to bear her up, solid as anything. "We need to find the Queen of Wands."

"Yes," said Niamh, and followed her.

Avery sighed, and turned to bow his head to the Lady. "We have to go," he said.

"Yes, you do," she agreed, and watched him as he rejoined his friends, forming a line of children, covered in crows, walking on the surface of the sea. It was an improbable thing, but no more so than anything else that had happened, and she was smiling as she turned away from them.

EPILOGUE

IN WHICH COURTS ARE MADE CLEAR

The Queen of Swords has a reputation for making monsters, and most of the Pages are monsters in their own way, but she does not forge most of them, nor have anything to do with their creation. Each ruler crafts their own Court, claiming them from the resources of their land. A Consort, when desired, Lord or Lady; a Knight, to carry their will across the protectorates; and, at times, a Page, who serves as living weapon for their regnant. Many Consorts will refuse to share space with a Page, for so many of them are monsters.

The Pages are heartless, all of them, even the kindest, you see. They act according to their own ideals, and not to the ideals of the gentle or the merciful. The Page of Frozen Waters is the worst of them, and always has been, having been crafted from ice and the drowned, but without the natural mercies to which those ordinary things are heir. And if the Page of Gentle Embers is the best of them, it is only because the Queen of Wands could envision no cruelty when she crafted her companion. They are not human. They are monsters, and that the Queen of Swords is forever blamed for the making of monsters when the Pages exist is one more piece of proof that the world is ever and always essentially unfair.

But all of them, once they have the scent of something to be destroyed, will return again and again, and to make an enemy of a Page is to make an enemy of the elements themselves, in their rawest, cruelest form.

Avery and Zib walked on, all unaware that both the wind and water were set against them now, in different ways, or that their journey was so very far from over as to be barely begun . . .